WEEP NOT MY WANTON

GW00457973

WEEP
NOT MY WANTON
Selected short stories

A E Coppard

TURNPIKE BOOKS

'Dusky Ruth', 'Weep not my Wanton', 'Adam & Eve & Pinch Me' first published in
Adam & Eve & Pinch Me (1921); 'The Wife of Ted Wickham' first published in *The
Black Dog* (1923); 'The Higgler' and 'The Watercress Girl' first published in
Fishmonger's Fiddle (1925); 'The Field of Mustard' first published in *The Field of Mustard*
(1926).

turnpikebooks@gmail.com

ISBN 9780957233621

Typeset by RefineCatch Ltd

Printed and bound by

CONTENTS

DUSKY RUTH

At the close of an April day, chilly and wet, the traveller came to a country town. In the Cotswolds, though the towns are small and sweet and the inns snug, the general habit of the land is bleak and bare. He had newly come upon upland roads so void of human affairs, so lonely, that they might have been made for some forgotten uses by departed men, and left to the unwitting passage of such strangers as himself. Even the unending walls, built of old rough laminated rock, that detailed the far-spreading fields, had grown very old again in their courses; there were dabs of darkness, buttons of moss, and fossils on every stone. He had passed a few neighbourhoods, sometimes at the crook of a stream, or at the cross of debouching roads, where old habitations, their gangrenated thatch riddled with bird holes, had not been so much erected as just spattered about the place. Beyond these signs an odd lark or blackbird, the ruckle of partridges, or the nifty gallop of a hare, had been the only mitigation of the living loneliness that was almost as profound by day as by night. But the traveller had a care for such times and places. There are men who love to gaze with the mind at things that can never be seen, feel at least the throb of a beauty that will never be known, and hear over immense bleak reaches the echo of that which is no celestial music, but only their own hearts' vain cries; and though his garments clung to him like clay it was with deliberate questing step that the traveller trod the single street of the town, and at last entered the inn, shuffling his shoes in the doorway for a moment and striking the raindrops from his hat. Then he turned into a small smoking-room. Leather-lined benches, much worn, were fixed to the wall under the window and in other odd corners and nooks behind mahogany tables. One wall was furnished with all the congenial gear of a bar, but without any intervening counter. Opposite a bright fire was burning, and a neatly dressed young woman sat before it in a Windsor chair, staring at the flames. There was no other inmate of the room, and as he entered the girl rose up and greeted him. He found that he could be accommodated for the night, and in a few moments his hat and scarf were removed and placed inside the fender, his wet overcoat was taken to the kitchen, the landlord, an old fellow, was lending him a roomy pair of slippers, and a maid was setting supper in an adjoining room.

He sat while this was doing and talked to the barmaid. She had a beautiful, but rather mournful face, as it was lit by the firelight, and when her glance was turned away from it her eyes had a piercing brightness. Friendly and well-spoken as she was, the melancholy in her aspect was noticeable – perhaps it was the dim room, or the wet day, or the long hours ministering a multitude of cocktails to thirsty gallantry.

When he went to his supper he found cheering food and drink, with pleasant garniture of silver and mahogany. There were no other visitors, he was to be alone; blinds were drawn, lamps lit, and the fire at his back was comforting. So he sat long about his meal until a white-faced maid came to clear the table, discoursing to him of country things as she busied about the room. It was a long narrow room, with a sideboard and the door at one end and the fireplace at the other. A bookshelf, almost devoid of books, contained a number of plates; the long wall that faced the windows was almost destitute of pictures, but there were hung upon it, for some inscrutable but doubtless sufficient reason, many dish-covers, solidly shaped, of the kind held in such mysterious regard and known as 'willow pattern'; one was even hung upon the face of a map. Two musty prints were mixed with them, presentments of horses having a stilted, extravagant physique and bestridden by images of inhuman and incommunicable dignity, clothed in whiskers, coloured jackets, and tight white breeches.

He took down the books from the shelf, but his interest was speedily exhausted, and the almanacs, the county directory, and various guide-books were exchanged for the *Cotswold Chronicle*. With this, having drawn the deep chair to the hearth, he whiled away the time. The newspaper amused him with its advertisements of stock shows, farm auctions, travelling quacks and conjurers, and there was a lengthy account of the execution of a local felon, one Timothy Bridger, who had murdered an infant in some shameful circumstances. This dazzling crescendo proved rather trying to the traveller; he threw down the paper.

The town was all quiet as the hills, and he could hear no sounds in the house. He got up and went across the hall to the smoke room. The door was shut, but there was light within, and he entered. The girl sat there much as he had seen her on his arrival, still alone, with feet on fender. He shut the door behind him, sat down, and crossing his legs puffed at his pipe, admired the snug little room and the pretty figure of the girl, which he could do without embarrassment as her meditative head, slightly bowed, was turned away from him. He could see something of her, too, in the mirror at the bar, which repeated also the agree-able contours of bottles of coloured wines and rich liqueurs – so entrancing in form and aspect that they seemed destined to charming histories, even in disuse – and those of familiar outline containing mere spirits or small beer, for which are reserved the harsher destinies of base oils, horse medicines, disinfectants, and cold tea. There were coloured glasses for bitter wines, white glasses for sweet, a tiny leaden sink beneath them, and the four black handles of the beer engine.

The girl wore a light blouse of silk, a short skirt of black velvet, and a pair of very thin silk stockings that showed the flesh of instep and shin so plainly that he could see they were reddened by the warmth of the fire. She had on a pair of dainty cloth shoes with high heels, but what was wonderful about her was the heap of rich black hair piled at the back of her head and shadowing the dusky neck. He sat puffing his pipe and letting the loud tick of the clock fill the quiet room. She did not stir and he could move no muscle. It was as if he had been willed to come there and wait silently. That, he felt now, had been his desire all the evening; and here, in her presence, he was more strangely stirred than by any event he could remember.

In youth he had viewed women as futile pitiable things that grew long hair, wore stays and garters, and prayed incomprehen-sible prayers. Viewing them in the stalls of the theatre from his vantage-point in the gallery, he always disliked the articulation of their naked shoulders. But still, there was a god in the sky, a god with flowing hair and exquisite eyes, whose one stride with an ardour grandly rendered took him across the whole round hemisphere to which his buoyant limbs were bound like spokes to the eternal rim and axle, his bright hair burning in the pity of the sunsets and tossing in the anger of the dawns.

Master traveller had indeed come into this room to be with this woman; she as surely desired him, and for all its accidental occasion it was as if he, walking the ways of the world, had suddenly come upon . . . what so imaginable with all permitted reverence as, well, just a shrine; and he, admirably humble, bowed the instant head.

Were there no other people within? The clock indicated a few minutes to nine. He sat on, still as stone, and the woman might have been of wax for all the movement or sound she made. There was allurement in the air between them; he had forborne his smoking, the pipe grew cold between his teeth. He waited for a look from her, a movement to break the trance of silence. No footfall in streets or house, no voice in the inn but the clock beating away as if pronouncing a doom. Suddenly it rasped out nine large notes, a bell in the town repeated them dolefully, and a cuckoo no farther than the kitchen mocked them with three times three. After that came the weak steps of the old landlord along the hall, the slam of doors, the clatter of lock and bolt, and then the silence returning unendurably upon them.

He arose and stood behind her; he touched the black hair. She made no movement or sign. He pulled out two or three combs, and dropping them into her lap let the whole mass tumble about his hands. It had a curious harsh touch in the unravelling, but was so full and shining; black as a rook's wings it was. He slid his palms through it. His fingers searched it and fought with its fine strangeness; into his mind there travelled a serious thought, stilling his wayward fancy – this was no wayward fancy, but a rite accomplished itself! (*Run, run, silly man, y'are lost!*) But having got so far he burnt his boats, leaned over, and drew her face back to him. And at that, seizing his wrists, she gave him back ardour for ardour, pressing his hands to her bosom, while the kiss was sealed and sealed again. Then she sprang up and picking his hat and scarf from the fender said:

'I have been drying them for you, but the hat has shrunk a bit, I'm sure – I tried it on.'

He took them from her and put them behind him; he leaned lightly back upon the table, holding it with both his hands behind him; he could not speak.

'Aren't you going to thank me for drying them?' she asked, picking her combs from the rug and repinning her hair.

'I wonder why we did that?' he asked, shamedly.

'It is what I'm thinking too,' she said.

'You were so beautiful about . . . about it, you know.'

She made no rejoinder, but continued to bind her hair, looking brightly at him under her brows. When she had finished she went close to him.

'Will that do?'

'I'll take it down again.'

'No, no, the old man or the old woman will be coming in.'

'What of that?' he said, taking her into his arms, 'tell me your name.'

She shook her head, but she returned his kisses and stroked his hair and shoulders with beautifully melting gestures.

'What is your name, I want to call you by your name?' he said; 'I can't keep calling you Lovely Woman, Lovely Woman.'

Again she shook her head and was dumb.

'I'll call you Ruth then, Dusky Ruth, Ruth of the black, beautiful hair.'

'That is a nice-sounding name – I knew a deaf and dumb girl named Ruth; she went to Nottingham and married an organ-grinder – but I should like it for my name.'

'Then I give it to you.'

'Mine is so ugly.'

'What is it?'

Again the shaken head and the burning caress.

'Then you shall be Ruth; will you keep that name?'

'Yes. If you give me the name I will keep it for you.'

Time had indeed taken them by the forelock, and they looked upon a ruddled world.

'I stake my one talent,' he said jestingly, 'and behold it returns me fortyfold; I feel like the boy who catches three mice with one piece of cheese.'

At ten o'clock the girl said:

'I must go and see how *they* are getting on,' and she went to the door.

'Are we keeping them up?'

She nodded.

'Are you tired?'

'No, I am not tired.'

She looked at him doubtfully.

'We ought not to stay in here; go into the coffee-room and I'll come there in a few minutes.'

'Right,' he whispered gaily, 'we'll sit up all night.'

She stood at the door for him to pass out, and he crossed the hall to the other room. It was in darkness except for the flash of the fire. Standing at the hearth he lit a match for the lamp, but paused at the globe; then he extinguished the match.

'No, it's better to sit in the firelight.'

He heard voices at the other end of the house that seemed to have a chiding note in them.

'Lord,' he thought, 'she is getting into a row?'

Then her steps came echoing over the stone floors of the hall; she opened the door and stood there with a lighted candle in her hand; he stood at the other end of the room, smiling.

'Good night,' she said.

'O no, no! come along,' he protested, but not moving from the hearth.

'Got to go to bed,' she answered.

'Are they angry with you?'

'No.'

'Well, then, come over here and sit down.'

'Got to go to bed,' she said again, but she had meanwhile put her candlestick upon the little sideboard and was trimming the wick with a burnt match.

'O, come along, just half an hour,' he protested. She did not answer but went on prodding the wick of the candle.

'Ten minutes, then,' he said, still not going towards her.

'Five minutes,' he begged.

She shook her head, and picking up the candlestick turned to the door. He did not move, he just called her name: 'Ruth!'

She came back then, put down the candlestick and tiptoed across the room until he met her. The bliss of the embrace was so poignant that he was almost glad when she stood up again and said with affected steadiness, though he heard the tremor in her voice:

'I must get you your candle.'

She brought one from the hall, set it on the table in front of him, and struck the match.

'What is my number?' he asked.

'Number six room,' she answered, prodding the wick vaguely with her match, while a slip of white wax dropped over the shoulder of the new candle. 'Number six . . . next to mine.'

The match burnt out; she said abruptly 'Good night,' took up her own candle and left him there.

In a few moments he ascended the stairs and went into his room. He fastened the door, removed his coat, collar, and slippers, but the rack of passion had seized him and he moved about with no inclination to sleep. He sat down, but there was no medium of distraction. He tried to read the newspaper which he had carried up with him, and without realizing a single phrase he forced himself to read again the whole account of the execution of the miscreant Bridger. When he had finished this he carefully folded the paper and stood up, listening. He went to the parting wall and tapped thereon with his finger tips. He waited half a minute, one minute, two minutes; there was no answering sign. He tapped again, more loudly, with his knuckles, but there was no response, and he tapped many times. He opened his door as noiselessly as possible; along the dark passage there were slips of light under the other doors, the one next his own, and the one beyond that. He stood in the corridor listening to the rumble of old voices in the farther room, the old man and his wife going to their rest. Holding his breath fearfully, he stepped to *her* door and tapped gently upon it. There was no answer, but he could somehow divine her awareness of him; he tapped again; she moved to the door and whispered 'No, no, go away.' He turned the handle, the door was locked.

'Let me in,' he pleaded. He knew she was standing there an inch or two beyond him.

'Hush,' she called softly. 'Go away, the old woman has ears like a fox.'

He stood silent for a moment.

'Unlock it,' he urged; but he got no further reply, and feeling foolish and baffled he moved back to his own room, cast his clothes from him, doused the candle and crept into the bed with soul as wild as a storm-swept forest, his heart beating a vagrant summons. The room filled with strange heat, there was no composure for mind or limb, nothing but flaming visions and furious embraces.

'Morality . . . what is it but agreement with your own soul?'

So he lay for two hours – the clocks chimed twelve – listening with foolish persistency for *her* step along the corridor, fancying every light sound – and the night was full of them – was her hand upon the door.

Suddenly – and then it seemed as if his very heart would abash the house with its thunder – he could hear distinctly someone knocking on the wall. He got quickly from his bed and stood at the door, listening. Again the knocking was heard, and having half-clothed himself he crept into the passage, which was now in utter darkness, trailing his hand along the wall until he felt her door; it was standing open. He entered her room and closed the door behind him. There was not the faintest gleam of light, he could see nothing. He whispered 'Ruth!' and she was standing there. She touched him, but not speaking. He put out his hands, and they met round her neck; her hair was flowing in its great wave about her; he put his lips to her face and found that her eyes were streaming with tears, salt and strange and disturbing. In the close darkness he put his arms about her with no thought but to comfort her; one hand had plunged through the long harsh tresses and the other across her hips before he realised that she was ungowned; then he was aware of the softness of her breasts and the cold naked sleekness of her shoulders. But she was crying there, crying silently with great tears, her strange sorrow stifling his desire.

'Ruth, Ruth, my beautiful dear!' he murmured soothingly. He felt for the bed with one hand, and turning back the quilt and sheets he lifted her in as easily as a mother does her child, replaced the bedding, and, in his clothes, he lay stretched beside her comforting her. They lay so, innocent as children, for an hour, when she seemed to have gone to sleep. He rose then and went silently to his room, full of weariness.

In the morning he breakfasted without seeing her, but as he had business in the world that gave him just an hour longer at the inn before he left it for good and all, he went into the smoke-room and found her. She greeted him with curious gaze, but merrily enough, for there were other men there now, farmers, a butcher, a registrar, an old, old man. The hour passed, but not these men, and at length he donned his coat, took up his stick, and said goodbye. Her shining glances followed him to the door, and from the window as far as they could view him.

WEEP NOT MY WANTON

Air and light on Sack Down at summer sunset were soft as oint-
ment and sweet as milk; at least, that is the notion the down
might give to a mind that bloomed within its calm horizons,
some happy victim of romance it might be, watching the silken
barley moving in its lower fields with the slow movement of
summer sea, reaching no harbour, having no end. The toilers
had mostly given over; their ploughs and harrows were left to
the abandoned fields; they had taken their wages and gone, or
were going, home; but at the crown of the hill a black barn stood
by the roadside, and in its yard, amid sounds of anguish, a score
of young boar pigs were being gelded by two brown lads and a
gipsy fellow. Not half a mile of distance here could enclose you
the compass of their cries. If a man desired peace he would step
fast down the hill towards Arwall with finger in ear until he
came to quiet at a bank overlooking slopes of barley, and could
perceive the fogs of June being born in the standing grass beyond.

Four figures, a labourer and his family, travelled slowly up the road proceeding across the hill, a sound mingling dully with their steps – the voice of the man. You could not tell if it were noise of voice or of footsteps that first came into your ear, but it could be defined on their advance as the voice of a man upbraiding his little son.

'You're a naughty, naughty – you're a vurry, *vurry* naughty boy! Oi can't think what's comen tyeh!'

The father towered above the tiny figure shuffling under his elbow, and kept his eyes stupidly fixed upon him. He saw a thin boy, a spare boy, a very shrunken boy of seven or eight years, crying quietly. He let no grief out of his lip, but his white face was streaming with dirty tears. He wore a man's cap, an unclean sailor jacket, large knickerbockers that made a mockery of his lean joints, a pair of women's button boots, and he looked straight ahead.

'The idear! To go and lose a sixpence like that then! Where dye think yer'll land yerself, ay? Wher'd I be if I kept on losing sixpences, ay? A creature like you, ay!' and lifting his heavy hand the man struck the boy a blow behind with shock enough to disturb a heifer. They went on, the child with sobs that you could feel rather than hear. As they passed the black barn the gipsy bawled encouragingly: 'Selp me, father, that's a good 'un, wallop his trousers!'

But the man ignored him, as he ignored the yell of the pig and the voice of the lark rioting above them all; he continued his litany:

'You're a naughty, naughty *boy*, an' I dunno what's comen tyeh!'

The woman, a poor slip of a woman she was, walked behind them with a smaller child: she seemed to have no desire to shield the boy or to placate the man. She did not seem to notice them, and led the toddling babe, to whom she gabbled, some paces in the rear of the man of anger. He was a great figure with a bronzed face; his trousers were tied at the knee, his wicker bag was slung over his shoulder. With his free and massive hand he held the hand of the boy. He was slightly drunk, and walked with his legs somewhat wide, at the beginning of each stride lifting his heel higher than was required, and at the end of it placing his foot firmly but obliquely inwards. There were two bright medals on the breast of his waistcoat, presumably for valour; he was perhaps a man who would stand upon his rights and his dignities, such as they were – but then he was drunk. His language, oddly unprofane, gave a subtle and mean point to his decline from the heroic standard. He only ceased his complaining to gaze swayingly at the boy; then he struck him. The boy, crying quietly, made no effort to avoid or resist him.

'You understand me, you bad boy! As long as you're with me you got to come under collar. And wher'll you be next I *dunno*, a bad creature like you, ay! An' then to turn roun' an' answer me! *I dunno!* I dunno *what's* comen tyeh. Ye know ye lost that sixpence through glammering about. Wher d'ye lose it, ay? Wher d'ye lose it, ay?'

At these questions he seized the boy by the neck and shook him as a child does a bottle of water. The baby behind them was taken with little gusts of laughter at the sight, and the woman cooed back playfully at her.

'George, George!' yelled the woman.

The man turned round.

'Look after Annie!' she yelled again.

'What's up?' he called.

Her only answer was a giggle of laughter as she disappeared behind a hedge. The child toddled up to its father and took his hand, while the quiet boy took her other hand with relief. She laughed up into their faces, and the man resumed his homily.

'He's a bad, bad boy. He's a vurry *naughty* bad boy!'

By and by the woman came shuffling after them; the boy looked furtively around and dropped his sister's hand.

'Carm on, me beauty!' cried the man, lifting the girl to his shoulder. 'He's a bad boy; you 'ave a ride on your daddy.' They went on alone, and the woman joined the boy. He looked up at her with a sad face.

'O, my Christ, Johnny!' she said, putting her arms round the boy, 'what's 'e bin doin' to yeh? Yer face is all blood!'

'It's only me nose, mother. Here,' he whispered, 'here's the tanner.'

They went together down the hill towards the inn, which had already a light in its windows. The screams from the barn had ceased, and a cart passed them full of young pigs, bloody and subdued. The hill began to resume its old dominion of soft sounds. It was nearly nine o'clock, and one anxious farmer still made hay although, on this side of the down, day had declined, and with a greyness that came not from the sky, but crept up from the world. From the quiet hill, as the last skein of cocks was carted to the stack, you could hear dimly men's voices and the rattle of their gear.

ADAM & EVE & PINCH ME

. . . and in the whole of his days, vividly at the end of the afternoon – he repeated it again and again to himself – the kind
country spaces had *never* absorbed *quite* so rich a glamour of
light, so miraculous a bloom of clarity. He could feel streaming
in his own mind, in his bones, the same crystalline brightness
that lay upon the land. Thoughts and images went flowing
through him as easily and amiably as fish swim in their pools;
and as idly, too, for one of his specutions took up the theme of
his family name. There was such an agreeable oddness about it,
just as there was about all the luminous sky today, that it touched
him as just a little remarkable. What *did* such a name connote,
signify, or symbolize? It was a rann of a name, but it had euphony!
Then again, like the fish, his ambulating fancy flashed into other
shallows, and he giggled as he paused, peering at the buds in the
brake. Turning back towards his house again he could see,
beyond its roofs, the spire of the church tinctured richly as the

vane: all round him was a new grandeur upon the grass of the
fields, and the spare trees had shadows below that seemed to
support them in the manner of a plinth, more real than them-
selves, and the dykes and any chance heave of the level fields
were underlined, as if for special emphasis, with long shades of
mysterious blackness.

With a little drift of emotion that had at other times assailed
him in the wonder and ecstasy of pure light, Jaffa Codling pushed
through the slit in the back hedge and stood within his own
garden. The gardener was at work. He could hear the voices of
the children about the lawn at the other side of the house. He
was very happy, and the place was beautiful, a fine white many-
windowed house rising from a lawn bowered with plots of mould,
turreted with shrubs, and overset with a vast walnut tree. This
house had deep clean eaves, a roof of faint coloured slates that,
after rain, glowed dully, like onyx or jade, under the red chim-
neys, and halfway up at one end was a balcony set with black
balusters. He went to a French window that stood open and
stepped into the dining room. There was no one within, and, on
that lonely instant, a strange feeling of emptiness dropped upon
him. The clock ticked almost as if it had been caught in some
indecent act; the air was dim and troubled after that glory
outside. Well, now, he would go up at once to his study and
write down for his new book the ideas and images he had accu-
mulated – beautiful rich thoughts they were – during that
wonderful afternoon. He went to mount the stairs and he was
passed by one of the maids; humming a silly song she brushed
past him rudely, but he was an easy-going man – maids were
unteachably tiresome – and reaching the landing he sauntered
towards his room. The door stood slightly open and he could
hear voices within. He put his hand upon the door . . . it would
not open any farther. What the devil . . . he pushed – like the

bear in the tale – and he pushed, and he pushed – was there something against it on the other side? He put his shoulder to it . . . some wedge must be there, and *that* was extraordinary. Then his whole apprehension was swept up and whirled as by an avalanche – Mildred, his wife, was in there; he could hear her speaking to a man in fair soft tones and the rich phrases that could be used only by a woman yielding a deep affection to him. Codling kept still. Her words burned on his mind and thrilled him as if spoken to himself. There was a movement in the room, then utter silence. He again thrust savagely at the partly open door, but he could not stir it. The silence within continued. He beat upon the door with his fists, crying, 'Mildred, Mildred!' There was no response, but he could hear the rocking armchair commence to swing to and fro. Pushing his hand round the edge of the door he tried to thrust his head between the opening. There was not space for this, but he could just peer into the corner of a mirror hung near, and this is what he saw: the chair at one end of its swing, a man sitting in it, and upon one arm of it Mildred, the beloved woman, with her lips upon the man's face, caressing him with her hands. Codling made another effort to get into the room – as vain as it was violent. 'Do you hear me, Mildred?' he shouted. Apparently neither of them heard him; they rocked to and fro while he gazed stupefied. What, in the name of God . . . What this . . . was she bewitched . . . were there such things after all as magic, devilry!

He drew back and held himself quite steadily. The chair stopped swaying, and the room grew awfully still. The sharp ticking of the clock in the hall rose upon the house like the tongue of some perfunctory mocker. Couldn't they hear the clock? . . . Couldn't they hear his heart? He had to put his hand upon his heart, for, surely, in that great silence inside there, they would hear its beat, growing so loud now that it seemed almost to stun him! Then in a queer way he found himself reflecting, observing, analysing his own actions and intentions. He found some of them to be just a little spurious, counterfeit. He felt it would be easy, so perfectly easy to flash in one blast of anger and annihilate the two. He would do nothing of the kind. There was no occasion for it. People didn't really do that sort of thing, or, at least, not with a genuine passion. There was no need for anger. His curiosity was satisfied, quite satisfied, he was certain, he had not the remotest interest in the man. A welter of unexpected thoughts swept upon his mind as he stood there. As a writer of books he was often stimulated by the emotions and impulses of other people, and now his own surprise was beginning to intrigue him, leaving him, O, quite unstirred emotionally, but interesting him profoundly.

He heard the maid come stepping up the stairway again, humming her silly song. He did not want a scene, or to be caught eavesdropping, and so turned quickly to another door. It was locked. He sprang to one beyond it; the handle would not turn. 'Bah! what's *up* with 'em?' But the girl was now upon him, carrying a tray of coffee things. 'O, Mary!' he exclaimed casually, 'I . . .' To his astonishment the girl stepped past him as if she did not hear or see him, tapped upon the door of his study, entered, and closed the door behind her. Jaffa Codling then got really angry. 'Hell! were the blasted servants in it!' He dashed to the door again and tore at the handle. It would not even turn, and, though he wrenched with fury at it, the room was utterly sealed against him. He went away for a chair with which to smash the effrontery of that door. No, he wasn't angry, either with his wife or this fellow – Gilbert, she had called him – who had a strangely familiar aspect as far as he had been able to take it in; but when one's servants . . . faugh!

The door opened and Mary came forth smiling demurely. He was a few yards farther along the corridor at that moment.

'Mary!' he shouted, 'leave the door open!' Mary carefully closed it and turned her back on him. He sprang after her with bad words bursting from him as she went towards the stairs and flitted lightly down, humming all the way as if in derision. He leaped downwards after her three steps at a time, but she trotted with amazing swiftness into the kitchen and slammed the door in his face. Codling stood, but kept his hands carefully away from the door, kept them behind him. 'No, no,' he whispered cunningly, 'there's something fiendish about door handles today, I'll go and get a bar, or a butt of timber,' and, jumping out into the garden for some such thing, the miracle happened to him. For it was nothing else than a miracle, the unbelievable, the impossible, simple and laughable if you will, but having as much validity as any miracle can ever invoke. It was simple and laugh-able because by all the known physical laws he should have collided with his gardener, who happened to pass the window with his wheelbarrow as Codling jumped out on to the path. And it was unbelievable that they should not, and impossible that they *did* not collide; and it was miraculous, because Codling stood for a brief moment in the garden path and the wheel-barrow of Bond, its contents, and Bond himself passed appar-ently through the figure of Codling as if he were so much air, as if he were not a living breathing man but just a common ghost. There was no impact, just a momentary breathlessness. Codling stood and looked at the retreating figure going on utterly unaware of him. It is interesting to record that Codling's first feelings were mirthful. He giggled. He was jocular. He ran along in front of the gardener, and let him pass through him once more; then after him again; he scrambled into the man's barrow, and was wheeled about by this incomprehensible thick-headed gardener who was dead to all his master's efforts to engage his attention. Presently he dropped the wheelbarrow and went away, leaving Codling to cogitate upon the occurrence. There was no room for doubt, some essential part of him had become detached from the obviously not less vital part. He felt he was essential because he was responding to the experience, he was reacting in the normal way to normal stimuli, although he happened for the time being to be invisible to his fellows and unable to communicate with them. How had it come about – this queer thing? How could he discover what part of him had cut loose, as it were? There was no question of this being death; death wasn't funny, it wasn't a joke; he had still all his human instincts. You didn't get angry with a faithless wife or joke with a fool of a gardener if you were dead, certainly not! He had realised enough of himself to know he was the usual man of instincts, desires, and prohibitions, complex and contradictory; his family history for a million or two years would have denoted that, not explicitly – obviously impossible – but suggestively. He had found himself doing things he had no desire to do, doing things he had a desire *not* to do, thinking thoughts that had no contiguous meanings, no meanings that could be related to his general experience. At odd times he had been chilled – aye, and even agreeably surprised – at the immense potential evil in himself. But still, this was no mere Jekyll and Hyde affair, that a man and his own ghost should separately inhabit the same world was a horse of quite another colour. The other part of him was alive and active somewhere . . . as alive . . . as alive . . . yes, as *he* was, but dashed if he knew where! What a lark when they got back to each other and compared notes! In his tales he had brooded over so many imagined personalities, followed in the track of so many psychological enigmas that he *had* felt at times a stranger to himself. What if, after all, that brooding had given him the faculty of projecting this figment of himself into the world of men. Or was he some unrealized latent element of being without its natural integument, doomed now to drift over the ridge of the world for ever. Was it his personality, his spirit? Then how was the dashed thing working? Here was he with the most wonderful happening in human experience, and he couldn't differentiate or disinter things. He was like a new Adam flung into some old Eden.

There was Bond tinkering about with some plants a dozen yards in front of him. Suddenly his three children came round from the other side of the house, the youngest boy leading them, carrying in his hand a small sword which was made, not of steel, but of some more brightly shining material; indeed it seemed at one moment to be of gold, and then again of flame, transmuting everything in its neighbourhood into the likeness of flame, the hair of the little girl Eve, a part of Adam's tunic; and the fingers of the boy Gabriel as he held the sword were like pale tongues of fire. Gabriel, the youngest boy, went up to the gardener and gave the sword into his hands, saying: 'Bond, is this sword any good?' Codling saw the gardener take the weapon and examine it with a careful sort of smile; his great gnarled hands became immediately transparent, the blood could be seen moving diligently about the veins. Codling was so interested in the sight that he did not gather in the gardener's reply. The little boy was dissatisfied and repeated his question, 'No, but Bond, is this sword any good?' Codling rose, and stood by invisible. The three beautiful children were grouped about the great angular figure of the gardener in his soiled clothes, looking up now into his face, and now at the sword, with anxiety in all their puckered eyes. 'Well, Marse Gabriel,' Codling could hear him reply, 'as far as a sword goes, it may be a good un, or it may be a bad un, but, good as it is, it can never be anything but a bad thing.' He then gave it back to them; the boy Adam held the haft of it, and the girl Eve rubbed the blade with curious fingers. The younger boy stood looking up at the gardener with unsatisfied gaze. 'But, Bond, *can't* you say if this sword's any *good?*' Bond turned to his spade and trowels. 'Mebbe the shape of it's wrong, Marse Gabriel, though it seems a pretty handy size.' Saying this he moved off across the lawn. Gabriel turned to his brother and sister and took the sword from them; they all followed after the gardener and once more Gabriel made inquiry: 'Bond, is this sword any *good?*' The gardener again took it and made a few passes in the air like a valiant soldier at exercise. Turning then, he lifted a bright curl from the head of Eve and cut it off with a sweep of the weapon. He held it up to look at it critically and then let it fall to the ground. Codling sneaked behind him and, picking it up, stood stupidly looking at it. 'Mebbe, Marse Gabriel,' the gardener was saying, 'it ud be better made of steel, but it has a smartish edge on it.' He went to pick up the barrow but Gabriel seized it with a spasm of anger, and cried out: 'No, no, Bond, will you say, just yes or no, Bond, is this sword any *good?*' The gardener stood still, and looked down at the little boy, who repeated his question – 'just yes or no, Bond!' 'No, Marse Gabriel!' 'Thank you, Bond,' replied the child with dignity, 'that's all we wanted to know,' and, calling to his mates to follow him, he ran away to the other side of the house.

Codling stared again at the beautiful lock of hair in his hand, and felt himself grow so angry that he picked up a strange looking flowerpot at his feet and hurled it at the retreating gardener. It struck Bond in the middle of the back and, passing clean through him, broke on the wheel of his barrow, but Bond seemed to be quite unaware of this catastrophe. Codling rushed after, and, taking the gardener by the throat, he yelled, 'Damn you, will you tell me what all this means?' But Bond proceeded calmly about his work un-noticing, carrying his master about as if he were a clinging vapour, or a scarf hung upon his neck. In a few moments,

Codling dropped exhausted to the ground. 'What . . . O Hell . . . what, what am I to do?' he groaned, 'What has happened to me? What shall I *do*? What *can* I do?' He looked at the broken flowerpot. 'Did I invent that?' He pulled out his watch. 'That's a real watch, I hear it ticking, and it's six o'clock.' Was he dead or disembodied or mad? What was this infernal lapse of identity? And who the devil, yes, who was it upstairs with Mildred? He jumped to his feet and hurried to the window; it was shut; to the door, it was fastened; he was powerless to open either. Well! well! this was experimental psychology with a vengeance, and he began to chuckle again. He'd have to write to McDougall about it. Then he turned and saw Bond wheeling acorss the lawn towards him again. '*Why* is that fellow always shoving that infernal green barrow around?' he asked, and, the fit of fury seizing him again, he rushed towards Bond, but, before he reached him, the three children danced into the garden again, crying, with great excitement, 'Bond, O, Bond!' The gardener stopped and set down the terrifying barrow; the children crowded about him, and Gabriel held out another shining thing, asking: 'Bond, is this box any good?' The gardener took the box and at once his eyes lit up with interest and delight. 'O, Marse Gabriel, where'd ye get it? Where'd ye get it?' 'Bond,' said the boy impatiently, 'is the box any *good*?' 'Any good?' echoed the man, 'Why, Marse Gabriel, Marse Adam, Miss Eve, look yere!' Holding it down in front of them, he lifted the lid from the box and a bright coloured bird flashed out and flew round and round above their heads. 'O,' screamed Gabriel with delight, 'it's a kingfisher!' 'That's what it is,' said Bond, 'a kingfisher!' 'Where?' asked Adam. 'Where?' asked Eve. 'There it flies – round the fountain – see it? see it!' 'No,' said Adam. 'No,' said Eve.

'O, do, do, see it,' cried Gabriel, 'here it comes, it's coming!' and, holding his hands on high, and standing on his toes, the child cried out as happy as the bird which Codling saw flying above them.

'I can't see it,' said Adam.

'Where is it, Gaby?' asked Eve.

'O, you stupids,' cried the boy. '*There* it goes. There it goes . . . there . . . it's gone!'

He stood looking brightly at Bond, who replaced the lid.

'What shall we do now?' he exclaimed eagerly. For reply, the gardener gave the box into his hand, and walked off with the barrow. Gabriel took the box over to the fountain. Codling, unseen, went after him, almost as excited as the boy; Eve and her brother followed. They sat upon the stone tank that held the falling water. It was difficult for the child to unfasten the lid; Codling attempted to help him, but he was powerless. Gabriel looked up into his father's face and smiled. Then he stood up and said to the others:

'Now, *do* watch it this time.'

They all knelt carefully beside the water. He lifted the lid and, behold, a fish like a gold carp, but made wholly of fire, leaped from the box into the fountain. The man saw it dart down into the water, he saw the water bubble up behind it, he heard the hiss that the junction of fire and water produces, and saw a little track of steam follow the bubbles about the tank until the figure of the fish was consumed and disappeared. Gabriel, in ecstasies, turned to his sister with blazing happy eyes, exclaiming:

'There! Evey!'

'What was it?' asked Eve, nonchalantly, 'I didn't see anything.'

'More didn't I,' said Adam.

'Didn't you see that lovely fish?'

'No,' said Adam.

'No,' said Eve.

'O, stupids,' cried Gabriel, 'it went right past the bottom of the water.'

'Let's get a fishin' hook,' said Adam.

'No, no, no,' said Gabriel, replacing the lid of the box. 'O, no.'

Jaffa Codling had remained on his knees staring at the water so long that, when he looked around him again, the children had gone away. He got up and went to the door, and that was closed; the windows, fastened. He went moodily to a garden bench and sat on it with folded arms. Dusk had begun to fall into the shrubs and trees, the grass to grow dull, the air chill, the sky to muster its gloom. Bond had overturned his barrow, stalled his tools in the lodge, and gone to his home in the village. A curious cat came round the house and surveyed the man who sat chained to his seven-horned dilemma. It grew dark and fearfully silent. Was the world empty now? Some small thing, a snail perhaps, crept among the dead leaves in the hedge, with a sharp, irritating noise. A strange flood of mixed thoughts poured through his mind until at last one idea disentangled itself, and he began thinking with tremendous fixity of little Gabriel. He wondered if he could brood or meditate, or 'will' with sufficient power to bring him into the garden again. The child had just vaguely recognized him for a moment at the waterside. He'd try that dodge, telepathy was a mild kind of a trick after so much of the miraculous. If he'd lost his blessed body, at least the part that ate and smoked and talked to Mildred . . . He stopped as his mind stumbled on a strange recognition . . . What a joke, of course . . . idiot . . . not to have seen *that*. He stood up in the garden with joy . . . of course, *he* was upstairs with Mildred, it was himself, the other bit of him, that Mildred had been talking to. What a howling fool he'd been.

He found himself concentrating his mind on the purpose of getting the child Gabriel into the garden once more, but it was with a curious mood that he endeavoured to establish this relationship. He could not fix his will into any calm intensity of power, or fixity of purpose, or pleasurable mental ecstasy. The utmost force seemed to come with a malicious threatening splenetic 'entreaty'. That damned snail in the hedge broke the thread of his meditation; a dog began to bark sturdily from a distant farm; the faculties of his mind became joggled up like a child's picture puzzle, and he brooded unintelligibly upon such things as skating and steam engines, and Elizabethan drama so lapped about with themes like jealousy and chastity. Really now, Shakespeare's Isabella was the most consummate snob in . . . He looked up quickly to his wife's room and saw Gabriel step from the window to the balcony as if he were fearful of being seen. The boy lifted up his hands and placed the bright box on the rail of the balcony. He looked up at the faint stars for a moment or two, and then carefully released the lid of the box. What came out of it and rose into the air appeared to Codling to be just a piece of floating light, but as it soared above the roof he saw it grow to be a little ancient ship, with its hull and fully set sails and its three masts all of faint primrose flame colour. It cleaved through the air, rolling slightly as a ship through the wave, in widening circles above the house, making a curving ascent until it lost the shape of a vessel and became only a moving light hurrying to some sidereal shrine. Codling glanced at the boy on the balcony, but in that brief instant something had happened, the ship had burst like a rocket and released three coloured drops of fire which came falling slowly, leaving beautiful grey furrows of smoke in their track. Gabriel leaned over the rail with outstretched palms, and, catching the green star and the blue one as they drifted down to him, he ran with a rill of laughter back into the house. Codling sprang forward just in time to catch the red star; it lay vividly blasting his own palm for a monstrous second, and then, slipping through, was gone. He stared at the ground, at the balcony, the sky, and then heard an exclamation . . . his wife stood at his side.

'Gilbert! How you frightened me!' she cried, 'I thought you were in your room; come along in to dinner.' She took his arm and they walked up the steps into the dining room together. 'Just a moment,' said her husband, turning to the door of the room. His hand was upon the handle, which turned easily in his grasp, and he ran upstairs to his room. He opened the door. The light was on, the fire was burning brightly, a smell of cigarette smoke about, pen and paper upon his desk, the Japanese book-knife, the gilt matchbox, everything all right, no one there. He picked up a book from his desk . . . *Monna Vanna*. His bookplate was in it – *Ex Libris – Gilbert Cannister*. He put it down beside the green dish; two yellow oranges were in the green dish, and two most deliberately green Canadian apples rested by their side. He went to the door and swung it backwards and forwards quite easily. He sat on his desk trying to piece the thing together, glaring at the print and the book-knife and the smart matchbox, until his wife came up behind him exclaiming: 'Come along, Gilbert!'

'Where are the kids, old man?' he asked her, and, before she replied, he had gone along to the nursery. He saw the two cots, his boy in one, his girl in the other. He turned whimsically to Mildred, saying, 'There *are* only two, *are* there?' Such a question did not call for reply, but he confronted her as if expecting some assuring answer. She was staring at him with her bright beautiful eyes.

'Are there?' he repeated.

'How strange you should ask me that now!' she said . . . 'If you're a very good man . . . perhaps . . .'

'Mildred!'

She nodded brightly.

He sat down in the rocking chair, but got up again saying to her gently – 'We'll call him Gabriel.'

'But, suppose–'

'No, no,' he said, stopping her lovely lips, 'I know all about him.' And he told her a pleasant little tale.

THE HIGGLER

I

On a cold April afternoon a higgler was driving across Shag
Moor in a two-wheeled cart.

H. WITLOW
Dealer in Poultry
DINNOP

was painted on the hood; the horse was of mean appearance but
notorious ancestry. A high upland common was this moor, two
miles from end to end, and full of furze and bracken. There were
no trees and not a house, nothing but a line of telegraph poles
following the road, sweeping with rigidity from north to south;
nailed upon one of them a small scarlet notice to stonethrowers
was prominent as a wound. On so high and wide a region as
Shag Moor the wind always blew, or if it did not quite blow

there was a cool activity in the air. The furze was always green
and growing, and, taking no account of seasons, often golden.
Here in summer solitude lounged and snoozed; at other times, as
now, it shivered and looked sinister.

Higglers in general are ugly and shrewd, old and hard, crafty
and callous, but Harvey Witlow, though shrewd, was not ugly;
he was hard but not old, crafty but not at all unkind. If you had
eggs to sell he would buy them, by the score he would, or by the
long hundred. Other odds and ends he would buy or do, paying
good bright silver, bartering a bag of apples, carrying your little
pig to market, or fetching a tree from the nurseries. But the
season was backward, eggs were scarce, trade was bad – by
crumps, it was indeed! – and as he crossed the moor Harvey
could not help discussing the situation with himself. 'If things
don't change, and change for the better and change soon, I can't
last and I can't endure it; I'll be damned and done, and I'll have
to sell,' he said, prodding the animal with the butt of his whip,
'this cob. And,' he said, as if in afterthought, prodding the foot-
board, 'this cart, and go back to the land. And I'll have lost my
fifty pounds. Well, that's what war does for you. It does it for
you, sir,' he announced sharply to the vacant moor, 'and it does
it for me. Fifty pounds! I was better off in the war. I was better
off working for farmers – much. But it's no good chattering about
it, it's the trick of life; when you get so far, then you can go and
order your funeral. Get along, Dodger!'

The horse responded briskly for a few moments.

'I tell ye,' said Harvey adjuring the ambient air, 'you can go
and order your funeral. Get along, Dodger!'

Again Dodger got along.

'Then there's Sophy, what about Sophy and me?'

He was not engaged to Sophy Daws, not exactly, but he was
keeping company with her. He was not pledged or affianced, he

was just keeping company with her. But Sophy, as he knew, not only desired a marriage with Mr Witlow, she expected it, and expected it soon. So did her parents, her friends, and everybody in the village, including the postman who didn't live in it but wished he did, and the parson who did live in it but wished he didn't.

'Well, that's damned and done, fair damned and done now, unless things take a turn, and soon, so it's no good chattering about it.'

And just then and there things did take a turn. He had never been across the moor before; he was prospecting for trade. At the end of Shag Moor he saw standing back on the common, fifty yards from the road, a neat square house set in a little farm. Twenty acres, perhaps. The house was girded by some white palings; beside it was a snug orchard in a hedge covered with blackthorn bloom. It was very green and pleasant in front of the house. The turf was cleared and closely cropped, some ewes were grazing and under the blackthorn, out of the wind, lay half a dozen lambs, but what chiefly moved the imagination of Harvey Witlow was a field on the far side of the house. It had a small rick-yard with a few small stacks in it; everything here seemed on the small scale, but snug, very snug; and in that field and yard were hundreds of fowls, hundreds, of good breed, and mostly white. Leaving his horse to sniff the greensward, the higgler entered a white wicket gateway and passed to the back of the house, noting as he did so a yellow wagon inscribed ELIZABETH SADGROVE. PRATTLE CORNER.

At the kitchen door he was confronted by a tall gaunt woman of middle age with a teapot in her hands.

'Afternoon, ma'am. Have you anything to sell?' began Harvey Witlow, tilting his hat with a confident affable air. The tall woman was cleanly dressed, a superior person; her hair was grey. She gazed at him.

'It's cold,' he continued. She looked at him as uncompre-
hendingly as a mouse might look at a gravestone.

'I'll buy any mottal thing, ma'am. Except trouble; I'm full up
wi' that already. Eggs? Fowls?'

'I've not seen you before,' commented Mrs Sadgrove a little
bleakly, in a deep husky voice.

'No, 'tis the first time as ever I drove in this part. To tell you
the truth, ma'am, I'm new to the business. Six months. I was in
the war a year ago. Now I'm trying to knock up a connection.
Difficult work. Things are very quiet.'

Mrs Sadgrove silently removed the lid of the teapot, inspected
the interior of the pot with an intent glance, and then replaced
the lid as if she had seen a black beetle there.

'Ah, well,' sighed the higgler. 'You've a neat little farm here,
ma'am.'

'It's quiet enough,' said she.

'Sure it is, ma'am. Very lonely.'

'And it's difficult work too.' Mrs Sadgrove almost smiled.

'Sure it is, ma'am; but you does it well, I can see. Oh, you've
some nice little ricks of corn, eh! I does well enough at the
dealing now and again, but it's teasy work and mostly I don't
earn enough to keep my horse in shoe leather.'

'I've a few eggs, perhaps,' said she.

'I could do with a score or two, ma'am, if you could let me
have 'em.'

'You'll have to come all my way if I do.'

'Name your own price, ma'am, if you don't mind trading with
me.'

'Mind! Your money's as good as my own, isn't it?'

'It must be, ma'am. That's meaning no disrespects to you,' the
young higgler assured her hastily, and was thereupon invited to
enter the kitchen.

A stone floor with two or three mats; open hearth with burning logs; a big dresser painted brown, carrying a row of white cups on brass hooks and shelves of plates overlapping each other like the scales of fish. A dark settle half hid a flight of stairs with a small gate at the top. Under the window a black sofa, deeply indented, invited you a little repellingly, and in the middle of the room stood a large table, exquisitely scrubbed, with one end of it laid for tea. Evidently a living-room as well as kitchen. A girl, making toast at the fire, turned as the higgler entered. Beautiful she was: red hair, a complexion like the inside of a nut, blue eyes, and the hands of a lady. He saw it all at once, jacket of bright green wool, black dress, grey stockings and shoes, and forgot his errand, her mother, his fifty pounds, Sophy – momentarily he forgot everything. The girl strangely stared at him. He was tall, clean-shaven, with a loop of black hair curling handsomely over one side of his brow.

'Good afternoon,' said Harvey Witlow, as softly as if he had entered a church.

'Some eggs, Mary,' Mrs Sadgrove explained. The girl laid down her toasting-fork. She was less tall than her mother, whom she resembled only enough for the relationship to be noted. Silently she crossed the kitchen and opened a door that led into a dairy. Two pans of milk were creaming on a bench there and on the flags were two great baskets filled with eggs.

'How many are there?' asked Mrs Sadgrove, and the girl replied: 'Fifteen score, I think.'

'Take the lot, higgler?'

'Yes, ma'am,' he cried eagerly, and ran out to his cart and fetched a number of trays. In them he packed the eggs as the girl handed them to him from the baskets. Mrs Sadgrove left them together. For a time the higgler was silent.

'No,' at length he murmured, 'I've never been this road before.'

There was no reply from Mary. Sometimes their fingers touched, and often, as they bent over the eggs, her bright hair almost brushed his face.

'It is a loneish spot,' he ventured again.

'Yes,' said Mary Sadgrove.

When the eggs were all transferred her mother came in again.

'Would you buy a few pullets, higgler?'

'Any number, ma'am,' he declared quickly. Any number; by crumps, the tide was turning! He followed the mother into the yard, and there again she left him, waiting. He mused about the girl and wondered about the trade. If they offered him ten thousand chickens, he'd buy them, somehow, he would! She had stopped in the kitchen. Just in there she was, just behind him, a few feet away. Over the low wall of the yard a fat black pony was strolling in a field of bright greensward. In the yard, watching him, was a young gander, and on a stone staddle beside it lay a dead thrush on its back, its legs stiff in the air. The girl stayed in the kitchen; she was moving about, though, he could hear her; perhaps she was spying at him through the window. Twenty million eggs he would buy if Mrs Sadgrove had got them. She was gone a long time. It was very quiet. The gander began to comb its white breast with its beak. Its three-toed feet were a most tender pink, shaped like wide diamonds, and at each of the three forward points there was a toe like a small blanched nut. It lifted one foot, folding the webs, and hid it under its wing and sank into a resigned meditation on one leg. It had a blue eye that was meek – it had two, but you could only see one at a time – a meek blue eye, set in a pink rim that gave it a dissolute air, and its beak had raw red nostrils as if it suffered from the damp. Altogether a beautiful bird. And in some absurd way it resembled Mrs Sadgrove.

'Would you sell that young gollan, ma'am?' Harvey inquired when the mother returned.

Yes, she would sell him, and she also sold him two dozen pullets. Harvey packed the fowls in a crate.

'Come on,' he cried cuddling the squawking gander in his arms, 'you needn't be afraid of me, I never kills anything afore Saturdays.'

He roped it by its leg to a hook inside his cart. Then he took out his bag of money, paid Mrs Sadgrove her dues, said 'Good day, ma'am, good day,' and drove off without seeing another sign or stitch of that fine young girl.

'Get along, Dodger, get along wi' you.' They went bowling along for nearly an hour, and then he could see the landmark on Dan'el Green's Hill, a windmill that never turned though it looked a fine competent piece of architecture, just beyond Dinnop.

Soon he reached his cottage and was chaffing his mother, a hearty buxom dame, who stayed at home and higgled with any chance callers. At this business she was perhaps more enlightened than her son. It was almost a misfortune to get into her clutches.

'How much you give for this?' he cried, eyeing with humorous contempt an object in a coop that was neither flesh nor rude red herring.

'Oh crumps,' he declared, when she told him, 'I am damned and done!'

"Go on with you, that's a good bird, I tell you, with a full heart, as will lay in a month.'

'I doubt it's a hen at all,' he protested. 'Oh, what a ravenous beak! Damned and done I am.'

Mrs Witlow's voice began indignantly to rise.

'Oh, well,' mused her son, 'it's thrifty perhaps. It ain't quite right, but it's not so wrong as to make a fuss about, especially as I be pretty sharp set. And if it's hens you want,' he continued triumphantly, dropping the crate of huddled fowls before her, 'there's hens for you; and a gander! There's a gander for you, if it's a gander you want.'

Leaving them all in his cottage yard he went and stalled the horse and cart at the inn, for he had no stable of his own. After supper he told his mother about the Sadgroves of Prattle Corner. 'Prettiest girl you ever seen, but the shyest mottal alive. Hair like a squirrel, lovely.'

'An't you got to go over and see Sophy tonight?' inquired his mother, lighting the lamp.

'Oh Lord, if I an't clean forgot that! Well, I'm tired, shan't go tonight. See her tomorrow.'

II

Mrs Sadgrove had been a widow for ten years – and she was glad of it. Prattle Corner was her property, she owned it and farmed it with the aid of a little old man and a large lad. The older this old man grew, and the less wages he received (for Elizabeth Sadgrove was reputed a 'grinder'), the more ardently he worked; the older the lad grew the less he laboured and the more he swore. She was thriving. She was worth money was Mrs Sadgrove. Ah! And her daughter Mary, it was clear, had received an education fit for a lord's lady; she had been at a seminary for gentlefolk's females until she was seventeen. Well, whether or no, a clock must run as you time it; but it wronged her for the work of a farm, it spoiled her, it completely deranged her for the work of a farm; and this was a pity and foolish, because some day the farm was coming to her as didn't know hay from a bull's foot.

All this, and more, the young higgler quickly learned, and plenty more he soon divined. Business began to flourish with him now; his despair was gone, he was established, he could look forward, to whatever it was he wanted to look forward, with equanimity and such pleasurable anticipation as the chances and charges of life might engender. Every week, and twice a week, he would call at the farm, and though these occasions had their superior business inducements they often borrowed a less formal tone and intention.

'Take a cup of tea, higgler?' Mrs Sadgrove would abruptly invite him; and he would drink tea and discourse with her for half an hour on barndoor ornithology, on harness, and markets, the treatment of swine, the wear and tear of gear. Mary, always present, was always silent, seldom uttering a word to the higgler; yet a certain grace emanated from her to him, an interest, a light, a favour, circumscribed indeed by some modesty, shyness, some inhibition, that neither of them had the wit or the opportunity to overcome.

One evening he pulled up at the white palings of Prattle Corner. It was a calm evening in May, the sun was on its downgoing, chaffinches and wrens sung ceaselessly. Mary in the orchard was heavily veiled; he could see her over the hedge, holding a brush in her gloved hands, and a bee skep. A swarm was clustered like a great gnarl on the limb of an apple tree. Bloom was thickly covering the twigs. She made several timid attempts to brush the bees into the skep, but they resented this.

'They knows if you be afraid of 'em,' bawled Harvey; 'I better come and give you a hand.'

When he took the skep and brush from her she stood like one helpless, released by fate from a task ill-understood and gracelessly waived. But he liked her shyness, her almost uncouth immobility.

'Never mind about that,' said Harvey, as she unfastened her veil, scattering the white petals that had collected upon it; 'when they kicks they hurts, but I've been stung so often that I'm 'nocolated against 'em. They knows if you be afraid of 'em.'

Wearing neither veil nor gloves he went confidently to the tree, and collected the swarm without mishap.

'Don't want to show no fear of them,' said Harvey. 'Nor of anything else, come to that,' he added with a guffaw, 'nor anybody.'

At that she blushed and thanked him very softly, and she did look straight and clearly at him.

Never anything beyond a blush and a thank you. When, in the kitchen or the parlour, Mrs Sadgrove sometimes left them alone together Harvey would try a lot of talk, blarneying talk or sensible talk, or talk about events in the world that was neither the one nor the other. No good. The girl's responses were ever brief and confused. Why was this? Again and again he asked himself that question. Was there anything the matter with her? Nothing that you could see; she was a bright and beautiful being. And it was not contempt, either, for despite her fright, her voicelessness, her timid eyes, he divined her friendly feeling for himself; and he would discourse to his own mother about her and her mother:

'They are well-up people, you know, well off, plenty of money and nothing to do with it. The farm's their own, freehold. A whole row of cottages she's got, too, in Smoorton Comfrey, so I heard; good cottages, well let. She's worth a few thousands, I warrant. Mary's beautiful. I took a fancy to that girl the first moment I see her. But she's very highly cultivated – and, of course, there's Sophy.'

To this enigmatic statement Mrs Witlow offered no response; but mothers are inscrutable beings to their sons, always.

Once he bought some trees of cherries from Mrs Sadgrove, and went on a July morning to pick the fruit. Under the trees Mary was walking slowly to and fro, twirling a clapper to scare away the birds. He stood watching her from the gateway. Among the bejewelled trees she passed, turning the rattle with a listless air, as if beating time to a sad music that only she could hear. The man knew that he was deeply fond of her. He passed into the orchard, bade her good morning, and, lifting his ladder into one of the trees nearest the hedge, began to pluck cherries. Mary moved slimly in her white frock up and down a shady avenue in the orchard waving the clapper. The brightness of sun and sky was almost harsh; there was a little wind that feebly lifted the despondent leaves. He had doffed his coat; his shirt was white and clean. The lock of dark hair drooped over one side of his forehead; his face was brown and pleasant, his bare arms brown and powerful. From his high perch among the leaves Witlow watched for the girl to draw near to him in her perambulation. Knavish birds would scatter at her approach, only to drop again into the trees she had passed. His soul had an immensity of longing for her, but she never spoke a word to him. She would come from the shade of the little avenue, through the dumb trees that could only bend to greet her, into the sunlight whose dazzle gilded her own triumphant bloom. Fine! Fine! And always as she passed his mind refused to register a single thought he could offer her, or else his tongue would refuse to utter it. But his glance never left her face until she had passed out of sight again, and then he would lean against the ladder in the tree, staring down at the ground, seeing nothing or less than nothing, except a field mouse climbing to the top of a coventry bush in the hedge below him, nipping off one thick leaf and descending with the leaf in its mouth. Sometimes Mary rested at the other end of the avenue; the clapper would be silent and she would not appear for – oh, hours! She never rested near the trees Witlow was denuding. The mouse went on ascending and descending, and Witlow filled his basket, and shifted his stand, and wondered.

At noon he got down and sat on the hedge bank to eat a snack of lunch. Mary had gone indoors for hers, and he was alone for awhile. Capriciously enough, his thoughts dwelt upon Sophy Daws. Sophy was a fine girl, too; not such a lady as Mary Sadgrove – oh lord, no! her father was a game-keeper! – but she was jolly and ample. She had been a little captious lately, said he was neglecting her. That wasn't true; hadn't he been busy? Besides, he wasn't bound to her in any sort of way, and of course he couldn't afford any marriage yet awhile. Sophy hadn't got any money, never had any. What she did with her wages – she was a parlourmaid – was a teaser! Harvey grunted a little, and said 'Well!' And that is all he said, and all he thought, about Sophy Daws, then, for he could hear Mary's clapper begin again in a corner of the orchard. He went back to his work. There at the foot of the tree were the baskets full of cherries, and those yet to be filled.

'Phew, but that's hot!' commented the man, 'I'm as dry as a rattle.'

A few cherries had spilled from one basket and lay on the ground. The little furry mouse had found them and was industriously nibbling at one. The higgler nonchalantly stamped his foot upon it, and kept it so for a moment or two. Then he looked at the dead mouse. A tangle of entrails had gushed from its whiskered muzzle.

He resumed his work and the clapper rattled on throughout the afternoon, for there were other cherry trees that other buyers would come to strip in a day or two. At four o'clock he was finished. Never a word had he spoken with Mary, or she with him. When he went over to the house to pay Mrs Sadgrove Mary stopped in the orchard scaring the birds.

'Take a cup of tea, Mr Witlow,' said Mrs Sadgrove; and then she surprisingly added, 'Where's Mary?'

'Still a-frightening the birds, and pretty well tired of that, I should think, ma'am.'

The mother had poured out three cups of tea.

'Shall I go and call her in?' he asked, rising.

'You might,' said she.

In the orchard the clappering had ceased. He walked all round, and in among the trees, but saw no sign of Mary; nor on the common, nor in the yard. But when he went back to the house Mary was there already, chatting at the table with her mother. She did not greet him, though she ceased talking to her mother as he sat down. After drinking his tea he went off briskly to load the baskets into the cart. As he climbed up to drive off Mrs Sadgrove came out and stood beside the horse.

'You're off now?' said she.

'Yes, ma'am; all loaded, and thank you.'

She glanced vaguely along the road he had to travel. The afternoon was as clear as wine, the greensward itself dazzled him; lonely Shag Moor stretched away, humped with sweet yellow furze and pilastered with its telegraph poles. No life there, no life at all. Harvey sat on his driving board, musingly brushing the flank of his horse with the trailing whip.

'Ever round this way on Sundays?' inquired the woman, peering up at him.

'Well, not in a manner of speaking, I'm not, ma'am,' he answered her.

The widow laid her hand on the horse's back, patting vaguely. The horse pricked up its ears, as if it were listening.

'If you are, at all, ever, you must look in and have a bit of dinner with us.'

'I will, ma'am, I will.'

'Next Sunday?' she went on.

'I will, ma'am, yes, I will,' he repeated, 'and thank you.'

'One o'clock?' The widow smiled up at him.

'At one o'clock, ma'am; next Sunday; I will, and thank you,' he said.

She stood away from the horse and waved her hand. The first tangible thought that floated mutely out of the higgler's mind as he drove away was: 'I'm damned if I ain't a-going it, Sophy!'

He told his mother of Mrs Sadgrove's invitation with an air of curbed triumph. 'Come round – she says. Yes – I says – I 'ull. That's right – she says – so do.'

III

On the Sunday morn he dressed himself gallantly. It was again a sweet unclouded day. The church bell at Dinnop had begun to ring. From his window, as he fastened his most ornate tie, Harvey could observe his neighbour's two small children in the next garden, a boy and girl clad for church-going and each carrying a clerical book. The tiny boy placed his sister in front of a henroost and, opening his book, began to pace to and fro before her, shrilly intoning: 'Jesus is the shepherd, ring the bell. Oh lord, ring the bell, am I a good boy? Amen. Oh lord, ring the bell.' The little girl bowed her head piously over her book. The lad then picked up from the ground a dish which had contained the dog's food, and presented it momentarily before the lilac bush, the rabbit in a hutch, the axe fixed in a chopping block, and then before his sister. Without lifting her peering gaze from her book she meekly dropped two pebbles in the plate, and the boy passed on, lightly moaning, to the clothes-line post and a cock scooping in some dust.

'Ah, the little impets!' cried Harvey Witlow. 'Here, Toby! Here, Margaret!' He took two pennies from his pocket and lobbed them from the window to the astonished children. As they stooped to pick up the coins Harvey heard the hoarse voice of neighbour Nathan, their father, bawl from his kitchen: 'Come on in, and shut that bloody door, d'y'ear!'

Harnessing his moody horse to the gig Harvey was soon bowling away to Shag Moor, and as he drove along he sang loudly. He had a pink rose in his buttonhole. Mrs Sadgrove received him almost affably, and though Mary was more shy than ever before, Harvey had determined to make an impression. During the dinner he fired off his bucolic jokes, and pleasant tattle of a more respectful and sober nature; but after dinner Mary sat like Patience, not upon a monument, but as if upon a rocking-horse, shy and fearful, and her mother made no effort to inspire her as the higgler did, unsuccessful though he was. They went to the pens to look at the pigs, and as they leaned against the low walls and poked the maudlin inhabitants, Harvey began, 'Reminds me, when I was in the war . . .'

'Were you in the war?' interrupted Mrs Sadgrove.

'Oh, yes, I was in that war, ah, and there was a pig. . . . Danger? Oh lord, bless me, it was a bit dangerous, but you never knew where it was or what it 'ud be at next; it was like the sword of Damockels. There was a bullet once come 'ithin a foot of my head, and it went through a board an inch thick, slap through that board.' Both women gazed at him apprehendingly. 'Why, I might 'a been killed, you know,' said Harvey, cocking his eye musingly at the weather-vane on the barn. 'We was in billets at St Gratien, and one day a chasseur came up – a French yoossar, you know – and he began talking to our sergeant. That was Hubert Luxter, the butcher: died a month or two ago of measles. But this yoossar couldn't speak English at all, and none of us chaps could make sense of him. I never could understand that lingo somehow, never; and though there was half a dozen of us chaps there, none of us were man enough for it neither. "Nil

compree," we says, "non compos." I told him straight, "You
ought to learn English," I said, "it's much easier than your kind
of bally chatter." So he kept shaping up as if he was holding a
rifle, and then he'd say "Fusee – bang!" and then he'd say
"cushion" – kept on saying "cushion". Then he gets a bit of
chalk and draws on the wall something that looks like a horrible
dog, and says "cushion" again.'

'Pig,' interjected Mary Sadgrove softly.

'Yes, yes!' ejaculated Harvey, 'so 'twas! Do you know any
French lingo?'

'Oh, yes,' declared her mother, 'Mary knows it very well.'

'Ah,' sighed the higgler, 'I don't, although I been to France.
And I couldn't do it now, not for luck nor love. You learnt it, I
suppose. Well, this yoossar wants to borrow my rifle, but of course
I can't lend him. So he taps on this horrible pig he'd drawn, and
then he taps on his own head, and rolls his eyes about dreadful!
"Mad?" I says. And that was it, that was it. He'd got a pig on his
little farm there what had gone mad, and he wanted us to come
and shoot it; he was on leave and he hadn't got any ammunition.
So Hubert Luxter he says, "Come on, some of you," and we all
goes with the yoossar and shot the pig for him. Ah, that was a
pig! And when it died it jumped a somersault just like a rabbit. It
had got the mange, and was mad as anything I ever see in my life;
it was full of madness. Couldn't hit him at all at first, and it
kicked up bobs-a-dying. "Ready, present, fire!" Hubert Luxter
says, and bang goes the six of us, and every time we missed him
he spotted us and we had to run for our lives.'

As Harvey looked up he caught a glance of the girl fixed on
him. She dropped her gaze at once and, turning away, walked off
to the house.

'Come and take a look at the meadow,' said Mrs Sadgrove to
him, and they went into the soft smooth meadow where the

black pony was grazing. Very bright and green it was, and very blue the sky. He sniffed at the pink rose in his buttonhole, and determined that come what might he would give it to Mary if he could get a nice quiet chance to offer it. And just then, while he and Mrs Sadgrove were strolling alone in the soft smooth meadow, quite alone, she suddenly, startlingly, asked him: 'Are you courting anybody?'

'Beg pardon, ma'am?' he exclaimed.

'You haven't got a sweetheart, have you?' she asked, most deliberately.

Harvey grinned sheepishly: 'Ha, ha, ha,' and then he said, 'no.'

'I want to see my daughter married,' the widow went on significantly.

'Miss Mary!' he cried.

'Yes,' said she; and something in the higgler's veins began to pound rapidly. His breast might have been a revolving cage and his heart a demon squirrel. 'I can't live for ever,' said Mrs Sadgrove, almost with levity, 'in fact, not for long, and so I'd like to see her settled soon with some decent understanding young man, one that could carry on here, and not make a mess of things.'

'But, but,' stuttered the understanding young man, 'I'm no scholar, and she's a lady. I'm a poor chap, rough, and no scholar, ma'am. But mind you . . .'

'That doesn't matter at all,' the widow interrupted, 'not as things are. You want a scholar for learning, but for the land . . .'

'Ah, that's right, Mrs Sadgrove, but . . .'

'I want to see her settled. This farm, you know, with the stock and things are worth nigh upon three thousand pounds.'

'You want a farmer for farming, that's true, Mrs Sadgrove, but when you come to marriage, well, with her learning and French and all that . . .'

'A sensible woman will take a man rather than a box of tricks any day of the week,' the widow retorted. 'Education may be a fine thing, but it often costs a lot of foolish money.'

'It do, it do. You want to see her settled?'

'I want to see her settled and secure. When she is twenty-five she comes into five hundred pounds of her own right.'

The distracted higgler hummed and haa'ed in his bewilderment as if he had just been offered the purchase of a dubious duck. 'How old is she, ma'am?' he at last huskily inquired.

'Two-and-twenty nearly. She's a good healthy girl, for I've never spent a pound on a doctor for her, and very quiet she is, and very sensible; but she's got a strong will of her own, though you might not think it or believe it.'

'She's a fine creature, Mrs Sadgrove, and I'm very fond of her. I don't mind owning up to that, very fond of her I am.'

'Well, think it over, take your time, and see what you think. There's no hurry, I hope, please God.'

'I shan't want much time,' he declared with a laugh, 'but I doubt I'm the fair right sort for her.'

'Oh, fair days, fair doings!' said she inscrutably, 'I'm not a long liver, I'm afraid.'

'God forbid, ma'am!' His ejaculation was intoned with deep gravity.

'No, I'm not a long-living woman.' She surveyed him with her calm eyes, and he returned her gaze. Hers was a long sallow face, with heavy lips. Sometimes she would stretch her features (as if to keep them from petrifying) in an elastic grin, and display her dazzling teeth; the lips would curl thickly, no longer crimson, but blue. He wondered if there were any sign of a doom registered upon her gaunt face. She might die, and die soon.

'You couldn't do better than think it over, then, eh?' she had a queer frown as she regarded him.

'I couldn't do worse than not, Mrs Sadgrove,' he said gaily.

They left it at that. He had no reason for hurrying away, and he couldn't have explained his desire to do so, but he hurried away. Driving along past the end of the moor, and peering back at the lonely farm where they dwelled amid the thick furze snoozing in the heat, he remembered that he had not asked if Mary was willing to marry him! Perhaps the widow took her agreement for granted. That would be good fortune, for otherwise how the devil was he to get round a girl who had never spoken half a dozen words to him! And never would! She was a lady, a girl of fortune, knew her French; but there it was, the girl's own mother was asking him to wed her. Strange, very strange! He dimly feared something, but he did not know what it was he feared. He had still got the pink rose in his buttonhole.

IV

At first his mother was incredulous; when he told her of the astonishing proposal she declared he was a joker; but she was soon as convinced of his sincerity as she was amazed at his hesitation. And even vexed: 'Was there anything the matter with this Mary?'

'No, no, no! She's quiet, very quiet indeed, I tell you, but a fine young woman, and a beautiful young woman. Oh, she's all right, right as rain, right as a trivet, right as ninepence. But there's a catch in it somewheres, I fear. I can't see through it yet, but I shall afore long, or I'd have the girl, like a shot I would. 'Tain't the girl, mother, it's the money, if you understand me.'

'Well, I don't understand you, certainly I don't. What about Sophy?'

'Oh lord!' He scratched his head ruefully.

'You wouldn't think of giving this the go-by for Sophy, Harvey, would you? A girl as you ain't even engaged to, Harvey, would you?'

'We don't want to chatter about that,' declared her son. 'I got to think it over, and it's going to tie my wool, I can tell you, for there's a bit of craft somewheres, I'll take my oath. If there ain't, there ought to be!'

Over the alluring project his decision wavered for days, until his mother became mortified at his inexplicable vacillation.

'I tell you,' he cried, 'I can't make tops or bottoms of it all. I like the girl well enough, but I like Sophy, too, and it's no good beating about the bush. I like Sophy, she's the girl I love; but Mary's a fine creature, and money like that wants looking at before you throw it away, love or no love. Three thousand pounds! I'd be a made man.'

And as if in sheer spite to his mother; as if a bushel of money lay on the doorstep for him to kick over whenever the fancy seized him; in short (as Mrs Witlow very clearly intimated) as if in contempt of Providence he began to pursue Sophy Daws with a new fervour, and walked with that young girl more than he was accustomed to, more than ever before; in fact, as his mother bemoaned, more than he had need to. It was unreasonable, it was a shame, a foolishness; it wasn't decent and it wasn't safe.

On his weekly visits to the farm his mind still wavered. Mrs Sadgrove let him alone; she was very good, she did not pester him with questions and entreaties. There was Mary with her white dress and her red hair and her silence; a girl with a great fortune, walking about the yard, or sitting in the room, and casting not a glance upon him. Not that he would have known it if she did, for now he was just as shy of her. Mrs Sadgrove often left them alone, but when they were alone he could not dish up a word for the pretty maid; he was dumb as a statue. If either she or her mother had lifted so much as a finger then there would have been an end to his hesitations or suspicions, for in Mary's presence the fine glory of the girl seized him incontinently; he was again full of a longing to press her lips, to lay down his doubts, to touch her bosom – though he could not think she would ever allow that! Not an atom of doubt about *her* ever visited him; she was unaware of her mother's queer project. Rather, if she became aware he was sure it would be the end of him. Too beautiful she was, too learned, and too rich. Decidedly it was his native cunning, and no want of love, that inhibited him. Folks with property did not often come along and bid you help yourself. Not very often! And throw in a grand bright girl, just for good measure as you might say. Not very often!

For weeks the higgler made his customary calls, and each time the outcome was the same; no more, no less. 'Some dodge,' he mused, 'something the girl don't know and the mother does.' Were they going bankrupt, or were they mortgaged up to the neck, or was there anything the matter with the girl, or was it just the mother wanted to get hold of him? He knew his own value if he didn't know his own mind, and his value couldn't match that girl any more than his mind could. So what *did* they want him for? Whatever it was Harvey Witlow was ready for it whenever he was in Mary's presence, but once away from her his own craftiness asserted itself: it was a snare, they were trying to make a mock of him!

But nothing could prevent his own mother mocking him, and her treatment of Sophy was so unbearable that if the heart of that dusky beauty had not been proof against all impediments, Harvey might have had to whistle for her favour. But whenever he was with Sophy he had only one heart, undivided and true, and certain as time itself.

'I love Sophy best. It's true enough I love Mary, too, but I love Sophy better. I know it; Sophy's the girl I must wed. It might not be so if I weren't all dashed and doddered about the money; I don't know. But I do know that Mary's innocent of all this craftiness; it's her mother trying to mogue me into it.'

Later he would be wishing he could only forget Sophy and do it. Without the hindrance of conscience he could do it, catch or no catch.

He went on calling at the farm, with nothing said or settled, until October. Then Harvey made up his mind, and without a word to the Sadgroves he went and married Sophy Daws and gave up calling at the farm altogether. This gave him some feeling of dishonesty, some qualm, and a vague unhappiness; likewise he feared the cold hostility of Mrs Sadgrove. She would be terribly vexed. As for Mary, he was nothing to her, poor girl; it was a shame. The last time he drove that way he did not call at the farm. Autumn was advancing, and the apples were down, the bracken dying, the furze out of bloom, and the farm on the moor looked more and more lonely, and most cold, though it lodged a flame-haired silent woman, fit for a nobleman, whom they wanted to mate with a common higgler. Crafty, you know, too crafty!

V

The marriage was a gay little occasion, but they did not go away for a honeymoon. Sophy's grandmother from a distant village, Cassandra Fundy, who had a deafness and a speckled skin, brought her third husband, Amos, whom the family had never seen before. Not a very wise man, indeed he was a common man, stooping like a decayed tree, he was so old. But he shaved every day and his hairless skull was yellow. Cassandra, who was yellow too, had long since turned into a fool; she did not shave, though she ought to have done. She was like to die soon, but everybody said old Amos would live to be a hundred; it was expected of him, and he, too, was determined.

The guests declared that a storm was threatening, but Amos Fundy denied it and scorned it.

'Thunder p'raps, but 'twill clear; 'tis only de pride o' der morning.'

'Don't you be a fool,' remarked his wife enigmatically, 'you'll die soon enough.'

'You must behold der moon,' continued the octogenarian; 'de closer it is to der wheel, de closer der rain; de furder away it is, de furder der rain.'

'You could pour that man's brains into a thimble,' declared Cassandra of her spouse, 'and they wouldn't fill it – he's deaf.'

Fundy was right; the day did clear. The marriage was made and the guests returned with the man and his bride to their home. But Fundy was also wrong, for storm came soon after and rain set in. The guests stayed on for tea, and then, as it was no better, they feasted and stayed till night. And Harvey began to think they never would go, but of course they couldn't and so there they were. Sophy was looking wonderful in white stockings and shiny shoes and a red frock with a tiny white apron. A big girl she seemed, with her shaken dark hair and flushed face. Grandmother Fundy spoke seriously, but not secretly to her.

'I've had my fourteen touch of children,' said Grandmother Fundy. 'Yes, they were flung on the mercy of God – poor little devils. I've followed most of 'em to the churchyard. You go slow, Sophia.'

'Yes, granny.'

'Why,' continued Cassandra, embracing the whole company, as it were, with her disclosure, 'my mother had me by some gentleman!'

The announcement aroused no response except sympathetic, and perhaps encouraging, nods from the women.

'She had me by some gentleman – she ought to ha' had a twal' month, she did!'

'Wasn't she ever married?' Sophy inquired of her grand-mother.

'Married? Yes, course she was,' replied the old dame, 'of course. But marriage ain't everything. Twice she was, but not to he, she wasn't.'

'Not to the gentleman?'

'No! Oh, no! He'd got money – bushels! Marriage ain't much, not with these gentry.'

'Ho, ho, that's a tidy come-up!' laughed Harvey.

'Who was that gentleman?' Sophia's interest was deeply engaged. But Cassandra Fundy was silent, pondering like a china image. Her gaze was towards the mantelpiece, where there were four lamps – but only one usable – and two clocks – but only one going – and a coloured greeting card a foot long with large letters KEEP SMILING adorned with lithographic honeysuckle.

'She's hard of hearing,' interpolated grandfather Amos, 'very hard, gets worse. She've a horn at home, big as that . . .' His eyes roved the room for an object of comparison, and he seized upon the fire shovel that lay in the fender. 'Big as that shovel. Crown silver it is, and solid, a beautiful horn, but' – he brandished the shovel before them – 'her won't use 'en.'

'Granny, who was that gentleman?' shouted Sophy. 'Did you know him?'

'No! no!' declared the indignant dame. 'I dunno ever his name, nor I don't want to. He took hisself off to Ameriky, and now he's in the land of heaven. I never seen him. If I had, I'd a given it to him properly; oh, my dear, not blayguarding him, you know, but just plain language! Where's your seven commandments?'

At last the rain abated. Peeping into the dark garden you could see the fugitive moonlight hung in a million raindrops in the black twigs of all sorts of bushes and trees, while along the cantle of the porch a line of raindrops hung, even and regular, as if they were nailheads made of glass. So all the guests departed, in one long staggering, struggling, giggling and guffawing body, into the village street. The bride and her man stood in the porch, watching and waving hands. Sophy was momentarily grieving: what a lot of trouble and fuss when you announced that henceforward you were going to sleep with a man because you loved him true! She had said goodbye to her grandmother Cassandra, to her father and her little sister. She had hung on her mother's breast, sighing an almost intolerable farewell to innocence – never treasured until it is gone, and thenceforward a pretty sorrow cherished more deeply than wider joys.

Into Harvey's mind, as they stood there at last alone, momentarily stole an image of a bright-haired girl, lovely, silent, sad, whom he felt he had deeply wronged. And he was sorry. He had escaped the snare, but if there had been no snare he might this night have been sleeping with a different bride. And it would have been just as well. Sophy looked but a girl with her blown hair and wet face. She was wiping her tears on the tiny apron. But she had the breasts of a woman and decoying eyes.

'Sophy, Sophy!' breathed Harvey, wooing her in the darkness.

'It blows and it rains, and it rains and it blows,' chattered the crumpled bride, 'and I'm all so bescambled I can't tell wet from windy.'

'Come, my love,' whispered the bridegroom, 'come in, to home.'

VI

Four or five months later the higgler's affairs had again taken a rude turn. Marriage, alas, was not all it might be; his wife and his mother quarrelled unendingly. Sometimes he sided with one and sometimes with the other. He could not yet afford to install his mother in a separate cottage, and therefore even Sophy had to admit that her mother-in-law had a right to be living there with them, the home being hers. Harvey hadn't bought much of it; and though he was welcome to it all now, and it would be exclusively his as soon as she died, still, it was her furniture, and you couldn't drive any woman (even your mother) off her own property. Sophy, who wanted a home of her own, was vexed and moody, and antagonistic to her man. Business, too, had gone down sadly of late. He had thrown up the Shag Moor round months ago; he could not bring himself to go there again, and he had not been able to square up the loss by any substantial new connections. On top of it all his horse died. It stumbled on a hill one day and fell, and it couldn't get up, or it wouldn't – at any rate, it didn't. Harvey thrashed it and coaxed it, then he cursed it and kicked it; after that he sent for a veterinary man, and the veterinary man ordered it to be shot. And it was shot. A great blow to Harvey Witlow was that. He had no money to buy another horse; money was tight with him, very tight; and so he had to hire at fabulous cost a decrepit nag that ate like a good one. It ate – well, it would have astonished you to see what that creature disposed of, with hay the price it was, and corn gone up to heaven nearly. In fact Harvey found that he couldn't stand the racket much longer, and as he could not possibly buy another it looked very much as if he was in queer street once more, unless he could borrow the money from some friendly person. Of course there were plenty of friendly persons, but they had no money, just as there were many persons who had the money but were not what you might call friendly; and so the higgler began to reiterate twenty times a day, and forty times a day, that he was entirely and absolutely damned and done. Things were thus very bad with him, they were at their worst – for he had a wife to keep now, as well as a mother, and a horse that ate like Satan, and worked like a gnat – when it suddenly came into his mind that Mrs Sadgrove was reputed to have a lot of money, and had no call to be unfriendly to him. He had his grave doubts about the size of her purse, but there could be no harm in trying so long as you approached her in a right reasonable manner.

For a week or two he held off from this appeal, but the grim spectre of destitution gave him no rest, and so, near the close of a wild March day he took his desperate courage and his cart and the decrepit nag to Shag Moor. Wild it was, though dry, and the wind against them, a vast turmoil of icy air strident and baffling. The nag threw up its head and declined to trot. Evening was but an hour away, the fury of the wind did not retard it, nor the clouds hasten it. Low down the sun was quitting the wrack of storm, exposing a jolly orb of magnifying fire that shone flush under eaves and through the casements of cottages, casting a pattern of lattice and tossing boughs upon the interior walls, lovelier than dreamed-of pictures. The heads of mothers and old dames were also imaged there, recognizable in their black shadows; and little children held up their hands between window and wall to make five-fingered shapes upon the golden screen. To drive on the moor then was to drive into blasts more dire. Darkness began to fall, and bitter cold it was. No birds to be seen, neither beast nor man; empty of everything it was except sound and a marvel of dying light, and Harvey Witlow of Dinnop with a sour old nag driving from end to end of it.

At Prattle Corner dusk was already abroad: there was just one shaft of light that broached a sharp-angled stack in the rickyard, an ark of darkness, along whose top the gads and wooden pins and tilted straws were miraculously fringed in the last glare. Hitching his nag to the palings he knocked at the door, and knew in the gloom that it was Mary who opened it and stood peering forth at him.

'Good evening,' he said, touching his hat.

'Oh!' the girl uttered a cry, 'Higgler! What do you come for?' It was the longest sentence she had ever spoken to him; a sad frightened voice.

'I thought,' he began, 'I'd call – and see Mrs Sadgrove. I wondered . . .'

'Mother's dead,' said the girl. She drew the door farther back, as if inviting him, and he entered. The door was shut behind him, and they were alone in darkness, together. The girl was deeply grieving. Trembling, he asked the question: 'What is it you tell me, Mary?'

'Mother's dead,' repeated the girl, 'all day, all day, all day.' They were close to each other, but he could not see her. All round the house the wind roved lamentingly, shuddering at doors and windows. 'She died in the night. The doctor was to have come, but he has not come all day,' Mary whispered, 'all day, all day. I don't understand; I have waited for him, and he has not come. She died, she was dead in her bed this morning, and I've been alone all day, all day, and I don't know what is to be done.'

'I'll go for the doctor,' he said hastily, but she took him by the hand and drew him into the kitchen. There was no candle lit; a fire was burning there, richly glowing embers, that laid a gaunt shadow of the table across a corner of the ceiling. Every dish on the dresser gleamed, the stone floor was rosy, and each smooth curve on the dark settle was shining like ice. Without invitation he sat down.

'No,' said the girl, in a tremulous voice, 'you must help me.' She lit a candle: her face was white as the moon, her lips were sharply red, and her eyes were wild. 'Come,' she said, and he followed her behind the settle and up the stairs to a room where there was a disordered bed, and what might be a body lying under the quilt. The higgler stood still staring at the form under the quilt. The girl, too, was still and staring. Wind dashed upon the ivy at the window and hallooed like a grieving multitude. A crumpled gown hid the body's head, but thrust from under it, almost as if to greet him, was her naked lean arm, the palm of the hand lying uppermost. At the foot of the bed was a large washing bowl, with sponge and towels.

'You've been laying her out! Yourself!' exclaimed Witlow. The pale girl set down the candle on a chest of drawers. 'Help me now,' she said, and moving to the bed she lifted the crumpled gown from off the face of the dead woman, at the same time smoothing the quilt closely up to the body's chin. 'I cannot put the gown on, because of her arm, it has gone stiff.' She shuddered, and stood holding the gown as if offering it to the man. He lifted that dead naked arm and tried to place it down at the body's side, but it rested and he let go his hold. The arm swung back to its former outstretched position, as if it still lived and resented that pressure. The girl retreated from the bed with a timorous cry.

'Get me a bandage,' he said, 'or something we can tear up.'

She gave him some pieces of linen.

'I'll finish this for you,' he brusquely whispered, 'you get along downstairs and take a swig of brandy. Got any brandy?'

She did not move. He put his arm around her and gently urged her to the door.

'Brandy,' he repeated, 'and light your candles.'

He watched her go heavily down the stairs before he shut the door. Returning to the bed he lifted the quilt. The dead body was naked and smelt of soap. Dropping the quilt he lifted the outstretched arm again, like cold wax to the touch and unpliant as a sturdy sapling, and tried once more to bend it to the body's side. As he did so the bedroom door blew open with a crash. It was only a draught of the wind, and a loose latch – Mary had opened a door downstairs, perhaps – but it awed him, as if some invisible looker were there resenting his presence. He went and closed the door, the latch had a loose hasp, and tiptoeing nerv- ously back he seized the dreadful arm with a sudden brutal energy, and bent it by thrusting his knee violently into the hollow of the elbow. Hurriedly he slipped the gown over the head and inserted the arm in the sleeve. A strange impulse of modesty stayed him for a moment: should he call the girl and let her complete the robing of the naked body under the quilt? That preposterous pause seemed to add a new anger to the wind, and again the door sprang open. He delayed no longer, but letting it remain open, he uncovered the dead woman. As he lifted the chill body the long outstretched arm moved and tilted like the boom of a sail, but crushing it to its side he bound the limb fast with the strips of linen. So Mrs Sadgrove was made ready for her coffin. Drawing the quilt back to her neck, with a gush of relief he glanced about the room. It was a very ordinary bedroom: bed, washstand, chest of drawers, chair, and two pictures – one of deeply religious import, and the other a little pink print, in a gilded frame, of a bouncing nude nymph recumbent upon a cloud. It was queer: a lot of people, people whom you wouldn't think it of, had that sort of picture in their bedrooms.

Mary was now coming up the stairs again, with a glass half full of liquid. She brought it to him.

'No, you drink it,' he urged, and Mary sipped the brandy.

'I've finished – I've finished,' he said as he watched her, 'she's quite comfortable now.'

The girl looked her silent thanks at him, again holding out the glass. 'No, sup it yourself,' he said; but as she stood in the dim light, regarding him with her strange gaze, and still offering the drink, he took it from her, drained it at a gulp and put the glass upon the chest, beside the candle. 'She's quite comfortable now. I'm very grieved, Mary,' he said with awkward kindness, 'about all this trouble that's come on you.'

She was motionless as a wax image, as if she had died in her steps, her hand still extended as when he took the glass from it. So piercing was her gaze that his own drifted from her face and took in again the objects in the room: the washstand, the candle on the chest, the little pink picture. The wind beat upon the ivy outside the window as if a monstrous whip were lashing its slaves.

'You must notify the registrar,' he began again, 'but you must see the doctor first.'

'I've waited for him all day,' Mary whispered, 'all day. The nurse will come again soon. She went home to rest in the night.' She turned towards the bed. 'She has only been ill a week.'

'Yes?' he lamely said. 'Dear me, it is sudden.'

'I must see the doctor,' she continued.

'I'll drive you over to him in my gig.' He was eager to do that.

'I don't know,' said Mary slowly.

'Yes, I'll do that, soon's you're ready. Mary,' he fumbled with his speech, 'I'm not wanting to pry into your affairs, or any thing as don't concern me, but how are you going to get along now? Have you got any relations?'

'No,' the girl shook her head, 'no.'

'That's bad. What was you thinking of doing? How has she left you – things were in a baddish way, weren't they?'

'Oh, no,' Mary looked up quickly. 'She has left me very well off. I shall go on with the farm; there's the old man and the boy – they've gone to a wedding today; I shall go on with it. She was so thoughtful for me, and I would not care to leave all this, I love it.'

'But you can't do it by yourself, alone?'

'No. I'm to get a man to superintend, a working bailiff,' she said.

'Oh!' And again they were silent. The girl went to the bed and lifted the covering. She saw the bound arm and then drew the quilt tenderly over the dead face. Witlow picked up his hat and found himself staring again at the pink picture. Mary took the candle preparatory to descending the stairs. Suddenly the higgler turned to her and ventured: 'Did you know as she once asked me to marry you?' he blurted.

Her eyes turned from him, but he guessed – he could feel that she *had* known.

'I've often wondered why,' he murmured, 'why she wanted that.'

'She didn't,' said the girl.

That gave pause to the man; he felt stupid at once, and roved his fingers in a silly way along the roughened nap of his hat.

'Well, she asked me to,' he bluntly protested.

'She knew,' Mary's voice was no louder than a sigh, 'that you were courting another girl, the one you married.'

'But, but,' stuttered the honest higgler, 'if she knew that why did she want for me to marry you?'

'She didn't,' said Mary again; and again, in the pause, he did silly things to his hat. How shy this girl was, how lovely in her modesty and grief!

'I can't make tops or bottoms of it,' he said; 'but she asked me, as sure as God's my maker.'

'I know. It was me, I wanted it.'

'You!' he cried, 'you wanted to marry me!'

The girl bowed her head, lovely in her grief and modesty. 'She was against it, but I made her ask you.'

'And I hadn't an idea that you cast a thought on me,' he murmured. 'I feared it was a sort of trick she was playing on me. I didn't understand, I had no idea that you knew about it even. And so I didn't ever ask you.'

'Oh, why not, why not? I was fond of you then,' whispered she. 'Mother tried to persuade me against it, but I was fond of you – then.'

He was in a queer distress and confusion: 'Oh, if you'd only tipped me a word, or given me a sort of look,' he sighed. 'Oh, Mary!'

She said no more, but went downstairs. He followed her and immediately fetched the lamps from his gig. As he lit the candles: 'How strange,' Mary said, 'that you should come back just as I most needed help. I am very grateful.'

'Mary, I'll drive you to the doctor's now.'

She shook her head; she was smiling.

'Then I'll stay till the nurse comes.'

'No, you must go. Go at once.'

He picked up the two lamps, and turning at the door said, 'I'll come again tomorrow.' Then the wind rushed into the room: 'Goodbye,' she cried, shutting the door quickly behind him.

He drove away into deep darkness, the wind howling his thoughts strange and bitter. He had thrown away a love, a love that was dumb and hid itself. By God, he had thrown away a fortune, too! And he had forgotten all about his real errand until now, forgotten all about the loan! Well, let it go; give it up. He would give up higgling; he would take on some other job; a bailiff, a working bailiff, that was the job that would suit him, a working bailiff. Of course there was Sophy; but still – Sophy!

THE WIFE OF TED WICKHAM

Perhaps it is a mercy we can't see ourselves as others see us. Molly Wickham was a remarkably pretty woman in days gone by; maybe she is wiser since she has aged, but when she was young she was foolish. She never seemed to realize it, but I wasn't deceived.

So said the cattle-dealer, a healthy looking man, massive, morose, and bordering on fifty. He did not say it to anybody in particular, for it was said – it was to himself he said it – privately, musingly, as if to soothe the still embittered recollection of a beauty that was foolish, a fondness that was vain.

Ted Wickham himself was silly, too, when he married her. Must have been extraordinarily touched to marry a little soft, religious, teetotal party like her, and him a great sporting cock of a man, just come into a public-house business that his aunt had left him, The Half Moon, up on the Bath Road. He always ate like an elephant, but she'd only the appetite of a scorpion. And what was worse, he was a true blood conservative while all her family were a set of radicals that you couldn't talk sense to: if you only so much as mentioned the name of Gladstone they would turn their eyes up to the ceiling as if he was a saint in glory. Blood is thicker than water, I know, but it's unnatural stuff to drink so much of. Grant their name was. They christened her Pamela, and as if that wasn't cruel enough they messed her initials up by giving her the middle name of Isabel.

But she was a handsome creature, on the small side, but sound as a roach and sweet as an apple tree in bloom. Pretty enough to convert Ted, and I thought she would convert him, but she was a cussed woman – never did what you would expect of her – and so she didn't even try. She gave up religion herself, gave it up altogether and went to church no more. That was against her inclination, but of course it was only right, for Ted never could have put up with that. Wedlock's one thing and religion's two: that's odd and even: a little is all very well if it don't go a long ways. Parson Twamley kept calling on her for a year or two afterwards, trying to persuade her to return to the fold – he couldn't have called oftener if she had owed him a hundred pound – but she would not hear of it, she would not go. He was not much of a parson, not one to wake anybody up, but he had a good delivery, and when he'd the luck to get hold of a sermon of any sense his delivery was very good, very good indeed. She would say, 'No, sir, my feelings aren't changed one bit, but I won't come to church any more, I've my private reasons.' And the parson would glare across at old Ted as if he were a Belzeboob, for Ted always sat and listened to the parson chattering to her. Never said a word himself, always kept his pipe stuck in his jaw. Ted never persuaded her in the least, just left it to her, and she would come round to his manner of thinking in the end, for though he never actually said it, she always knew what his way of thinking was. A strange thing, it takes a real woman to do that, silly or no! At election times she would plaster the place all over with Tory bills, do it with her own hands!

Still, there's no stability in meekness of that sort, a weathervane can only go with wind and weather, and there was no sense in her giving in to Ted as she did, not in the long run, for he couldn't help but despise her. A man wants something or other to whet the edge of his life on; and he did despise her, I know.

But she was a fine creature in her way, only her way wasn't his. A beautiful woman, too, well limbered up, with lovely hair, but always a very proper sort, a milksop – Ted told me once that he had never seen her naked. Well, can you wonder at the man? And always badgering him to do things that could not be done at the time. To have The Half Moon painted, or enlarged, or insured: she'd keep on badgering him, and he could not make her see that any god's amount of money spent on paint wouldn't improve the taste of liquor.

'I can see as far into a quart pot as the King of England,' he says, 'and I know that if this bar was four times as big as 'tis a quart wouldn't hold a drop more then than it does now.'

'No, of course,' she says.

'Nor a drop less neither,' says Ted. He showed her that all the money expended on improvements and insurance and such things were so much off something else. Ted was a generous chap – liked to see plenty of everything, even though he had to give some of it away. But you can't make some women see some things.

'Not a roof to our heads, nor a floor to our feet, nor a pound to turn round on if a fire broke out,' Molly would say.

'But why should a fire break out?' he'd ask her. 'There never has been a fire here, there never ought to be a fire here, and what's more, there never will be a fire here, so why should there be a fire?'

And of course she let him have his own way, and they never had a fire there while he was alive, though I don't know that any great harm would have been done anyways, for after a few years trade began to slacken off, and the place got dull, and what with the taxes it was not much more than a bread and cheese business. Still, there's no matter of that: a man don't ask for a bed of roses: a world without some disturbance or anxiety would be like a duck-pond where the ducks sleep all day and are carried off at night by the foxes.

Molly was like that in many things, not really contrary, but no tact. After Ted died she kept on at The Half Moon for a year or two by herself, and regular as clockwork every month Pollock, the insurance manager, would drop in and try for to persuade her to insure the house or the stock or the furniture, any mortal thing. Well, believe you, when she had only got herself to please in the matter that woman wouldn't have anything to say to that insurance – she never did insure, and never would.

'I wouldn't run such a risk; upon my soul it's flying in the face of possibilities, Mrs Wickham' – he was a palavering chap, that Pollock; a tall fellow with sandy hair, and he always stunk of liniment for he had asthma on the chest – 'A very grave risk, it is indeed,' he would say, 'the Meazers' family was burnt clean out of hearth and home last St Valentine's day, and if they hadn't taken up a policy what would have become of those Meazers?'

'I dunno,' Molly says – that was the name Ted give her – 'I dunno, and I'm sorry for unfortunate people, but I've my private reasons.'

She was always talking about her private reasons, and they must have been devilish private, for not a soul on God's earth ever set eyes on them.

'Well, Mrs Wickham,' says Pollock, 'they'd have been a tidy ways up Queer Street, and ruin's a long-lasting affair,' Pollock says. He was a rare palavering chap, and he used to talk about Gladstone, too, for he knew her family history; but that didn't move her, and she did not insure.

'Yes, I quite agree,' she says, 'but I've my private reasons.'

Sheer female cussedness! But where her own husband couldn't persuade her Pollock had no chance at all. And then, of course, two years after Ted died she did go and have a fire there. The Half Moon was burnt clean out, rafters and railings, and she had to give it up and shift into the little bullseye business where she is now, selling bullseyes to infants and ginger beer to boy scholars on biycles. And what does it all amount to? Why, it don't keep her in hairpins. She had the most beautiful hair once. But that's telling the story back foremost.

Ted was a smart chap, a particular friend of mine (so was Molly), and he could have made something of himself and of his business, perhaps, if it hadn't been for her. He was a sportsman to the backbone; cricket, shooting, fishing, always game for a bit of life, any mortal thing – what was there he couldn't do? And a perfect demon with women, I've never seen the like. If there was a woman for miles around as he couldn't come at, then you could bet a crown no one else could. He had the gift. Well, when one woman ain't enough for a man, twenty ain't too many. He and me were in a tight corner together more than once, but he never went back on a friend, his word was his Bible oath. And there was he all the while tied up to this soft wife of his, who never once let on she knew of it at all, though she knowed much. And never would she cast the blink of her eyes – splendid eyes they were, too – on any willing stranger, nor even a friend, say, like myself; it was all Ted this and Ted that, though I was just her own age and Ted was twelve years ahead of us both. She didn't know her own value, wouldn't take her opportunities, hadn't the sense, as I say, though she had got everything else. Ah, she was a woman to be looking at once, and none so bad now; she wears well.

But she was too pious and proper, it aggravated him, but Ted never once laid a finger on her and never uttered one word of reproach though he despised her; never grudged her a thing in reason when things were going well with him. It's God Almighty's own true gospel – they never had a quarrel in all the twelve years they was wed, and I don't believe they ever had an angry word, but how he kept his hands off her I don't know. I couldn't have done it, but I was never married – I was too independent for that work. He'd contradict her sometimes, for she *would* talk, and Ted was one of your silent sorts, but *she* – she would talk for ever more. She was so artful that she used to invent all manners of tomfoolery on purpose to make him contradict her; believe you, she did, even on his death bed.

I used to go and sit with him when he was going, poor Ted, for I knew he was done for; and on the day he died, she said to him – and I was there and I heard it, 'Is there anything you would like me to do, dear?' And he said, 'No.' He was almost at his last gasp, he had strained his heart, but she was for ever on at him, even then, an unresting woman. It was in May, I remember it, a grand bright afternoon outside, but the room itself was dreadful, it didn't seem to be afternoon at all; it was unbearable for a strong man to be dying in such fine weather, and the carts going by, and though we were a watching him, it seemed more as if something was watching us.

And she says to him again: 'Isn't there anything you would like me to do?'

Ted says to her: 'Ah! I'd like to hear you give one downright good-damn curse. Swear, my dear!'

'At what?' she says.

'Me, if you like.'

'What for?' she says. I can see her now, staring at him.

'For my sins.'

'What sins?' she says.

Now did you ever hear anything like that? What sins! After a while she began at him once more.

'Ted, if anything happens to you I'll never marry again.'

'Do what you like,' says he.

'I'll not do that,' she says, and she put her arms round him, 'for you'd not rest quiet in your grave, would you, Ted?'

'Leave me alone,' he says, for he was a very crusty sick man, very crusty, poor Ted, but could you wonder? 'You leave me alone and I'll rest sure enough.'

'You can be certain,' she cries, 'that I'd never, never do that, I'd never look at another man after you, Ted, never; I promise it solemnly.'

"Don't bother me, don't bother at all.' And poor Ted give a grunt and turned over on his side to get away from her.

At that moment some gruel boiled over on the hob – gruel and brandy was all he could take. She turned to look after it, and just then old Ted gave a breath and was gone, dead. She turned like a flash, with the steaming pot in her hand, bewildered for a moment. She saw he had gone. Then she put the pot back gently on the fender, walked over to the window and pulled down the blind. Never dropped a tear, not one tear.

Well, that was the end of Ted. We buried him, one or two of us. There was an insurance on his life for fifty pounds, but Ted had long before mortgaged the policy and so there was next to nothing for her. But what else could the man do? (Molly always swore the bank defrauded her!) She put a death notice in the paper, how he was dead, and the date, and what he died of: 'after a long illness, nobly and patiently borne.' Of course, that was sarcasm, she never meant one word of it, for he was a terror to nurse, the worst that ever was; a strong man on his back is like a wasp in a bottle. But every year, when the day comes round – and it's ten years now since he died – she puts a memorial notice in the same paper about her loving faithful husband and the long illness nobly and patiently borne!

And then, as I said, the insurance man and the parson began to call again on that foolish woman, but she would not alter her ways for any of them. Not one bit. The things she had once enjoyed before her marriage, the things she had wanted her own husband to do but were all against his grain, these she could nohow bring herself to do when he was dead and gone and she was alone and free to do them. What a farce human nature can be! There was an Italian hawker came along with rings in his ears and a coloured cart full of these little statues of Cupid, and churches with spires a yard long and red glass in them, and heads of some of the great people like the Queen and General Gordon.

'Have you got a head of Lord Beaconsfield?' Molly asks him.

He goes and searches in his cart and brings her out a beautiful head on a stand, all white and new, and charges her half a crown for it. Few days later the parson calls on the job of persuading her to return to his flock now that she was free to go once more. But no. She says: 'I can never change now, sir, it may be all wrong of me, but what my man thought was good enough for me, and I somehow cling to that. It's all wrong, I suppose, and you can't understand it, sir, but it's all my life.'

Well, Twamley chumbled over an argument or two, but he couldn't move her; there's no mortal man could ever move that woman except Ted – and he didn't give a damn.

'Well,' says parson, 'I have hopes, Mrs Wickham, that you will come to see the matter in a new light, a little later on perhaps. In fact, I'm sure you will, for look, there's that bust,' he says, and he points to it on the mantelpiece. 'I thought you and he were all against Gladstone, but now you've got his bust upon your shelf; it's a new one, I see.'

'No, no, that isn't Gladstone,' cried Molly, all of a tremble, 'that isn't Gladstone, it's Lord Beaconsfield!'

'Indeed, but pardon me, Mrs Wickham, that is certainly a bust of Mr Gladstone.'

So it was. This Italian chap had deceived the silly creature and palmed her off with any bust that come handy, and it happened to be Gladstone. She went white to the teeth, and gave a sort of scream, and dashed the little bust in a hundred pieces on the hearth in front of the minister there. O, he had a very vexing time with her.

That was years ago. And then came the fire, and then the bullseye shop. For ten years now I've prayed that woman to marry me, and she just tells me: No. She says she pledged her solemn word to Ted as he lay a-dying that she would not wed again. It was his last wish – she says. But it's a lie, a lie, for I heard them both. Such a lie! She's a mad woman, but fond of him still in her way, I suppose. She liked to see Ted make a fool of himself, liked him better so. Perhaps that's what she don't see in me. And what I see in her – I can't imagine. But it's a something, something in her that sways me now just as it swayed me then, and I doubt but it will sway me for ever.

THE WATERCRESS GIRL

WHEN Mary McDowall was brought to the assize court the place was crowded, Mr. O'Kane said, 'inside out'. It was a serious trial, as everybody – even the prisoner – well knew; twelve tons of straw had been thrown down on the roads outside the hall to deaden the noise of carts passing and such-like pandemoniums, and when the judge drove up in his coach with jockeys on the horses, a couple of young trumpeters from the barracks stiffened on the steps and blew a terrible fanfare up into heaven. 'For a sort of a warning, I should think,' said Mr. O'Kane.

The prisoner's father having been kicked by a horse was unable to attend the trial, and so he had enlisted Mr. O'Kane to go and fetch him the news of it; and Mr. O'Kane in obliging his friend suffered annoyances and was abused in the court itself by a great fat geezer of a fellow with a long staff. 'If you remained on your haunches when the judge came in,' complained Mr. O'Kane, 'you were poked up, and if you stood up to get a look at the prisoner when *she* came in you were poked down. Surely to God we didn't go to look at the judge!'

Short was her trial, for the evidence was clear, and the guilt not denied. Prisoner neither sorrowed for her crime nor bemoaned her fate; passive and casual she stood there at the willing of the court for a thing she had done, and there were no tears now in Mary McDowall. Most always she dressed in black, and she was in black then, with masses of black hair; a pale face with a dark mole on the chin, and rich red lips; a big girl of twenty-five, not coarsely big, and you could guess she was strong. A passionate girl, caring nothing or not much for this justice; unimpressed by the solemn court, nor moved to smile at its absurdities; for all that passion concerns with is love – or its absence – love that gives its only gift by giving all. If you could have read her mind, not now but in its calm before the stress of her misfortune, you would have learned this much, although she herself could not have formulated it: I will give to love all it is in me to give; I shall desire of love all I can ever dream of and receive.

And because another woman had taken what Mary McDowall wanted, Mary had flung a corrosive acid in the face of her enemy, and Elizabeth Plantney's good looks were gone, gone for certain and for ever. So here was Mary McDowall and over there was Frank Oppidan; not a very fine one to mislead the handsome girl in the dock, but he had done it, and he too had suffered and the women in court had pity for him, and the men – envy. Tall, with light oiled hair and pink sleepy features (a pink heart, too, you might think, though you could not see it), he gave evidence against her in a nasal tone with a confident manner, and she did not waste a look on him. A wood-turner he was, and for about four years had 'kept company' with the prisoner, who lived near a village a mile or two away from his home. He had often urged her to marry him, but she would not, so a little while ago he told her he was going to marry Elizabeth Plantney. A few evenings later he had been strolling with Elizabeth Plantney on the road outside the town. It was not yet dark, about eight o'clock, but they had not observed the prisoner, who must have been dogging them, for she came slyly up and passed by them, turned, splashed something in his companion's face and then walked on. She didn't run; at first they thought it was some stupid joke, and he was for going after the prisoner whom he had recognized.

'I was mad angry,' declared Oppidan, 'I could have choked her. But Miss Plantney began to scream that she was blinded and burning, and I had to carry and drag her some ways back along the road until we came to the first house, Mr. Blackfriar's, where they took her in and I ran off for the doctor.' The witness added savagely, 'I wish I *had* choked her.'

There was full corroboration, prisoner had admitted guilt, and the counsel briefed by her father could only plead for a lenient sentence. A big man he was with a drooping yellow moustache and terrific teeth; his cheeks and hands were pink as salmon.

'Accused,' he said, 'is the only child of Fergus McDowall. She lives with her father, a respectable widower, at a somewhat retired cottage in the valley of Trinkel, assisting him in the conduct of his business – a small-holding by the river where he cultivates watercress, and keeps bees and hens and things of that kind. The witness Oppidan had been in the habit of cycling from his town to the McDowall's home to buy bunches of watercress, a delicacy of which, in season, he seems to have been – um – inordinately fond, for he would go twice, thrice and often four times a week. His visits were not confined to the purchase of watercress, and he seems to have made himself agreeable to the daughter of the house; but I am in possession of no information as to the nature of their intercourse beyond that

tendered by the witness Oppidan. Against my advice the prisoner, who is a very reticent, even a remarkable, woman, has
insisted on pleading guilty and accepting her punishment
without any – um – chance of mitigation, in a spirit, I hope, of
contrition, which is not – um – entirely unadmirable. My Lord,
I trust . . .'

While the brutal story was being recounted, the prisoner had
stood with closed eyes, leaning her hands upon the rail of the
dock; stood and dreamed of what she had not revealed:

Of her father Fergus McDowall; his child she was, although
he had never married. That much she knew, but who her mother
had been he never told her, and it did not seem to matter; she
guessed rather than knew that at her birth she had died, or soon
afterwards, and the man had fostered her. He and she had always
been together, alone, ever since she could remember, always
together, always happy, he was so kind; and so splendid in the
great boots that drew up to his thighs when he worked in the
watercress beds, cutting bunches deftly, or cleaning the weeds
from the water. And there were her beehives, her flock of hens,
the young pigs, and a calf that knelt and rubbed its neck on the
rich mead with a lavishing movement just as the ducks did when
the grass was dewy. She had seen the young pigs, no bigger than
rabbits, race across the patch of greensward to the blue-roan calf
standing nodding in the shade; they would prowl beneath the
calf, clustering round its feet, and begin to gnaw the calf's hoof
until, full of patience, she would gently lift her leg and shake it,
but would not move away. Save for a wildness of mood that
sometimes flashed through her, Mary was content, and loved the
life that she could not know was lonely with her father beside
the watercress streams. He was uncommunicative, like Mary,
but as he worked he hummed to himself or whistled the soft
tunes that at night he played on the clarinet. Tall and strong, a

handsome man. Sometimes he would put his arms around her
and say, 'Well, my dear.' And she would kiss him. She had
vowed to herself that she would never leave him, but then –
Frank had come. In this mortal conflict we seek not only that
pleasure may not divide us from duty, but that duty may not
detach us from life. He was not the first man or youth she could
or would have loved, but he was the one who had wooed her;
first-love's enlightening delight, in the long summer eves, in
those enticing fields! How easily she was won! All his offers of
marriage she had put off with the answer: 'No, it would never do
for me,' or 'I shall never marry', but then, if he angrily swore or
accused her of not loving him enough, her fire and freedom
would awe him almost as much as it enchanted. And she might
have married Frank if she could only have told him of her
dubious origin, but whether from some vagrant modesty, loyalty
to her father, or some reason whatever, she could not bring
herself to do that. Often these steady refusals enraged her lover,
and after such occasions he would not seek her again for weeks,
but in the end he always returned, although his absences grew
longer as their friendship lengthened. Ah, when the way to your
lover is long, there's but a short cut to the end. Came a time
when he did not return at all and then, soon, Mary found she
was going to have a child. 'Oh, I wondered where you were,
Frank, and why you were there, wherever it was, instead of
where I could find you.' But the fact was portentous enough to
depose her grief at his fickleness, and after a while she took no
further care or thought for Oppidan, for she feared that like her
own mother she would die of her child. Soon these fears left her
and she rejoiced. Certainly she need not scruple to tell him of
her own origin now, he could never reproach her now. Had he
come once more, had he come then, she would have married
him. But although he might have been hers for the lifting of a

finger, as they say, her pride kept her from calling him into the trouble, and she did not call him and he never sought her again. When her father realized her condition he merely said 'Frank?' and she nodded.

The child was early born, and she was not prepared; it came and died. Her father took it and buried it in the garden. It was a boy, dead. No one else knew, not even Frank, but when she was recovered her pride wavered and she wrote a loving letter to him, still keeping her secret. Not until she had written three times did she hear from him, and then he only answered that he should not see her any more. He did not tell her why, but she knew. He was going to marry Elizabeth Plantney, whose parents had died and left her £500. To Mary's mind that presented itself as a treachery to their child, the tiny body buried under a beehive in the garden. That Frank was unaware made no difference to the girl's fierce mood; it was treachery. Maternal anger stormed in her breast, it could only be allayed by an injury, a deep admonishing injury to that treacherous man. In her sleepless nights, the little crumpled corpse seemed to plead for this much, and her own heart clamoured, just as those bees murmured against him day by day.

So then she got some vitriol. Rushing past her old lover on the night of the crime she turned upon him with the lifted jar, but the sudden confrontation dazed and tormented her; in momentary hesitation she had dashed the acid, not into *his* faithless eyes, but at the prim creature linked to his arm. Walking away, she heard the crying of the wounded girl. After a while she had turned back to the town and given herself up to the police.

To her mind, as she stood leaning against the dock rail, it was all huddled and contorted, but that was her story set in its order. The trial went droning on beside her remembered grief like a dull stream neighbouring a clear one, two parallel streams that would meet in the end, were meeting now, surely, as the judge began to speak. And at the crisis, as if in exculpation, she suffered a whisper to escape her lips, though none heard it.

' 'Twas him made me a parent, but he was never a man himself. He took advantage; it was mean, I love Christianity.' She heard the judge deliver her sentence: for six calendar months she was to be locked in a gaol. 'O Christ!' she breathed, for it was the lovely spring; lilac, laburnum, and father wading the brooks in those boots drawn up to his thighs to rake the dark sprigs and comb out the green scum.

They took her away. 'I wanted to come out then,' said Mr. O'Kane, 'for the next case was only about a contractor defrauding the corporation – good luck to him, but he got three years – and I tried to get out of it, but if I did that geezer with the stick poked me down and said I'd not to stir out of it till the court rose. I said to him I'd kill him, but there was a lot of peelers about so I suppose he didn't hear it.'

II

Towards the end of the year Oppidan had made up his mind what he would do to Mary McDowall when she came out of prison. Poor Liz was marred for life, spoiled, cut off from the joys they had intended together. Not for all the world would he marry her now; he had tried to bring himself to that issue of chivalry, of decency, but it was impossible; he had failed in the point of grace. No man could love Elizabeth Plantney now, Frank could not visit her without shuddering, and she herself, poor generous wretch, had given him back his promise. Apart from his ruined fondness for her, they had planned to do much with the £500; it was to have set him up in a secure and easy way of trade, they would have been established in a year or two as

solid as a rock. All that chance was gone, no such chance ever
came twice in a man's lifetime, and he was left with Liz upon his
conscience. He would have to be kind to her for as long as he
could stand it. That was a disgust to his mind for he wanted to
be faithful. Even the most unstable man wishes he had been
faithful – but to which woman he is never quite sure. And then
that bitch Mary McDowall would come out of her prison and be
a mockery to him of what he had forgone, of what he had been
deprived. Savagely he believed in the balance wrought by an act
of vengeance – he, too! – eye for eye, tooth for tooth; it had a
threefold claim, simplicity, relief, triumph. The McDowall girl,
so his fierce meditations ran, miked in prison for six months and
then came out no worse than when she went in. It was no
punishment at all, they did no hurt to women in prison; the
court hadn't set wrong right at all, it never did; and he was a
loser whichever way he turned. But there was still a thing he
could do (Jove had slumbered, he would steal Jove's lightning)
and a project lay troubling his mind like a gnat in the eye, he
would have no peace until it was wiped away.

On an October evening, then, about a week after Mary
McDowall's release, Oppidan set off towards Trinkel. Through
Trinkel he went and a furlong past it until he came to their lane.
Down the lane too, and then he could hear the water ruttling
over the cataracts of the cress-beds. Not yet in winter, the year's
decline was harbouring splendour everywhere. Whitebeam was
a dissolute tangle of rags covering ruby drops, the service trees
were sallow as lemons, the oak resisted decay, but most confident of all were the tender-tressed ashes. The man walked
quietly to a point where, unobserved, he could view the
McDowall dwelling, with its overbowering walnut tree littering
the yard with husks and leaves, its small adjacent field with
banks that stooped in the glazed water. The house was heavy

and small, but there were signs of grace in the garden, of thrift in
the orderly painted sheds. The conical peak of a tiny stack was
pitched in the afterglow, the elms sighed like tired old matrons,
wisdom and content lingered here. Oppidan crept along the
hedges until he was in a field at the back of the house, a hedge
still hiding him. He was trembling. There was a light already in
the back window; one leaf of the window stood open and he saw
their black cat jump down from it into the garden and slink
away under some shrubs. From his standpoint he could not see
into the lighted room, but he knew enough of Fergus's habits to
be sure he was not within; it was his day for driving into the
town. Thus it could only be Mary who had lit that lamp. Trembling still! Just beyond him was a heap of dung from the stable,
and a cock was standing silent on the dunghill while two hens,
a white one and a black, bickered around him over some voided
grains. Presently the cock seized the black hen and the white
scurried away; but though his grasp was fierce and he bit at her
red comb, the black hen went on gobbling morsels from the
manure heap, and when at last he released her she did not
intermit her steady pecking. Then Oppidan was startled by a
flock of starlings that slid across the evening with the steady
movement of a cloud; the noise of their wings was like showers
of rain upon trees.

'Wait till it's darker,' he muttered, and skulking back to the
lane he walked sharply for half a mile. Then, slowly, he returned.
Unseen, he reached the grass that grew under the lighted
window, and stooped warily against the wall; one hand rested on
the wall, the other in his pocket. For some time he hesitated but
he knew what he had to do and what did it matter! He stepped
in front of the window.

In a moment, and for several moments longer, he was rigid
with surprise. It was Mary all right (the bitch!), washing her

hair, drying it in front of the kitchen fire, the thick locks pouring over her face as she knelt with her hands resting on her thighs. So long was their black flow that the ends lay in a small heap inside the fender. Her bodice hung on the back of a chair beside her, and her only upper clothing was a loose and disarrayed chemise that did not hide her bosom. Then, gathering the hair in her hands, she held the tresses closer to the fire, her face peeped through, and to herself she was smiling. Dazzling fair were her arms and the one breast he astonishingly saw. It was Mary; but not the Mary, dull ugly creature, whom his long rancour had conjured for him. Lord, what had he forgotten! Absence and resentment had pared away her loveliness from his recollection, but this was the old Mary of their passionate days, transfigured and marvellous.

Stepping back from the window into shadow again, he could feel his heart pound like a frantic hammer; every pulse was hurrying at the summons. In those breathless moments, Oppidan gazed as it were at himself, or at his mad intention, gazed wonderingly, ashamed and awed. Fingering the thing in his pocket, turning it over as a coin whose toss has deceived him, he was aware of a revulsion; gone revenge, gone rancour, gone all thought of Elizabeth, and there was left in his soul what had not gone and could never go. A brute she had been – it was bloody cruelty – but, but . . . but what? Seen thus, in her innocent occupation, the grim fact of her crime had somehow thrown a conquering glamour over her hair, the pale pride of her face, the intimacy of her bosom. Her very punishment was a triumph; on what account had she suffered if not for love of him? He could feel that chastening distinction meltingly now; she had suffered for his love.

There and then shrill cries burst upon them. The cat leaped from the garden to the window-sill; there was a thrush in its mouth, shrieking. The cat paused on the sill, furtive and hesitant. Without a thought Oppidan plunged forward, seized the cat and with his free hand clutched what he could of the thrush. In a second the cat released it and dropped into the room, while the crushed bird fluttered away to the darkened shrubs, leaving its tail feathers in the hand of the man.

Mary sprang up and rushed to the window. 'Is it you?' was all she said. Hastily she left the window, and Oppidan with a grin saw her shuffling into her bodice. One hand fumbled at the buttons, the other unlatched the door. 'Frank.' There was neither surprise nor elation. He walked in. Only then did he open his fist and the thrush's feathers floated in the air and idled to the floor. Neither of them remembered any more of the cat or the bird.

In silence they stood, not looking at each other.

'What do you want?' at length she asked. 'You're hindering me.'

'Am I?' he grinned. His face was pink and shaven, his hair was almost as smooth as a brass bowl. 'Well, I'll tell you.' His hat was cumbering his hands, so he put it carefully on the table.

'I come here wanting to do a bad thing, I own up to that. I had it in my mind to serve you same as you served her – you know who I mean. Directly I knew you had come home, that's what I meant to do. I been waiting about out there a good while until I saw you. And then I saw you. I hadn't seen you for a long, long time, and somehow, I dunno, when I saw you . . .'

Mary was standing with her hands on her hips; the black cascades of her hair rolled over her arms; some of the strands were gathered under her fingers, looped to her waist; dark weeping hair.

'I didn't mean to harm her!' she burst out. 'I never meant that for her, not what I did. Something happened to me that I'd not told you of then, and it doesn't matter now, and I shall never tell you. It was you I wanted to put a mark on, but directly I was in front of you I went all swavy, and I couldn't. But I had to throw it, I had to throw it.'

He sat down on a chair, and she stared at him across the table: 'All along it was meant for you, and that's God's truth.'

'Why?' he asked. She did not give him an answer then, but stood rubbing the fingers of one hand on the finely scrubbed boards of the table, tracing circles and watching them vacantly. At last, she put a question:

'Did you get married soon?'

'No,' he said.

'Aren't you? But of course it's no business of mine.'

'I'm not going to marry her.'

'Not?'

'No, I tell you I wouldn't marry her for five thousand pounds, nor for fifty thousand, I wouldn't.' He got up and walked up and down before the fire. 'She's – aw! You don't know, you don't know what you done to her! She'd frighten you. It's rotten, like a leper. A veil on indoors and out, has to wear it always. She don't often go out, but whether or no, she must wear it. Ah, it's cruel.'

There was a shock of horror as well as the throb of tears in her passionate compunction. 'And you're not marrying her!'

'No,' he said bluntly, 'I'm not marrying her.'

Mary covered her face with her hands, and stood quivering under her dark weeping hair.

'God forgive me, how pitiful I'm shamed!' Her voice rose in a sharp cry. 'Marry her, Frank! Oh, you marry her now, you must!'

'Not for a million, I'd sooner be in my grave.'

'Frank Oppidan, you're no man, no man at all. You never had the courage to be strong, nor the courage to be evil; you've only the strength to be mean.'

'O, dry up!' he said testily; but something overpowered her and she went leaning her head sobbing against the chimneypiece.

'Come on, girl!' he was instantly tender, his arms were around her, he had kissed her.

'Go your ways!' She was loudly resentful. 'I want no more of you.'

'It's all right, Mary. Mary, I'm coming to you again, just as I used to.'

'You . . .' She swung out of his embrace. 'What for? D'ye think I want you now? Go off to Elizabeth Plantney . . .' She faltered. 'Poor thing, poor thing, it shames me pitiful; I'd sooner have done it to myself. O, I wish I had.'

With a meek grin Oppidan took from his pocket a bottle with a glass stopper. 'Do you know what that is?'

It looked like a flask of scent. Mary did not answer. 'Sulphuric,' continued he, 'same as you threw at her.'

The girl silently stared while he moved his hand as if he were weighing the bottle. 'When I saw what a mess you'd made of her, I reckoned you'd got off too light, it ought to have been seven years for you. I only saw it once, and my inside turned right over, you've no idea. And I thought: there's she – done for. Nobody could marry her, less he was blind. And there's you, just a six months and out you come right as ever. That's how I thought and I wanted to get even with you then, for her sake, not for mine, so I got this, the same stuff, and I came thinking to give you a touch of it.'

Mary drew herself up with a sharp breath. 'You mean – throw it at me?'

'That's what I meant, honour bright, but I couldn't – not now.' He went on weighing the bottle in his hand.

'O, throw it, throw it!' she cried in bitter grief, but covering her face with her hands – perhaps in shame, perhaps fear.

'No, no, no, no.' He slipped the bottle back into his pocket. 'But why did you do it? She wouldn't hurt a fly. What good could it do you?'

'Throw it,' she screamed, 'throw it, Frank, let it blast me!'

'Easy, easy now. I wouldn't even throw it at a rat. See!' he cried. The bottle was in his hand again as he went to the open window and withdrew the stopper. He held it outside while the fluid bubbled to the grass; the empty bottle he tossed into the shrubs.

He sat down, his head bowed in his hands, and for some time neither spoke. Then he was aware that she had come to him, was standing there, waiting. 'Frank,' she said softly, 'there's something I got to tell you.' And she told him about the babe.

At first he was incredulous. No, no, that was too much for him to stomach! Very stupid and ironical he was until the girl's pale sincerity glowed through the darkness of his unbelief: 'You don't believe! How could it not be true!'

'But I can't make heads or tails of it yet, Mary. You a mother, and I were a father!' Eagerly and yet mournfully he brooded. 'If I'd 'a' known – I can't hardly believe it, Mary – so help me God, if I'd 'a' known . . .'

'You could 'a' done nothing, Frank.'

'Ah, but I'd 'a' known! A man's never a man till that's come to him.'

'Nor a woman's a woman, neither; that's true, I'm different now.'

'I'd 'a' been his father, I tell you. Now I'm nothing. I didn't know of his coming, I never see, and I didn't know of his going, so I'm nothing still.'

'You kept away from me. I was afraid at first and I wanted you, but you was no help to me, you kept away.'

'I'd a right to know, didn't I? You could 'a' wrote and told me.'

'I did write to you.'

'But you didn't tell me nothing.'

'You could 'a' come and see me,' she returned austerely, 'then you'd known. How could I write down a thing like that in a letter as anybody might open? Any dog or devil could play tricks with it when you was boozed or something.'

'I ought 'a bin told, I ought 'a bin told.' Stubbornly he maintained it. ' 'Twasn't fair, you.'

' 'Twasn't kind, you. You ought to 'a' come; I asked you, but you was sick o' me, Frank, sick o' me and mine. I didn't want any help, neither, 'twasn't that I wanted.'

'Would you 'a' married me then?' Sharply but persuasively he probed for what she neither admitted nor denied. 'Yes, yes, you would, Mary. 'Twould 'a' bin a scandal if I'd gone and married someone else.'

When at last the truth about her own birth came out between them, O, how ironically protestant he was! 'God a' mighty, girl, what did you take me for! There's no sense in you. I'll marry you now, for good and all (this minute if we could), honour bright, and you know it, for I love you always and always. You were his mother, Mary, and I were his father! What was he like, that little son?'

Sadly the girl mused. 'It was very small.'

'Light hair?'

'No, like mine, dark it was.'

'What colour eyes?'

She drew her fingers down through the long streams of hair. 'It never opened its eyes.' And her voice moved him so that he cried out: 'My love, my love, life's before us; there's a many good fish in the sea. When shall us marry?'

'Let me go, Frank. And you'd better go now, you're hindering me, and father will be coming in, and . . . and . . . the cakes are burning!'

Snatching up a cloth she opened the oven door and an odour of caraway rushed into the air. Inside the oven was a shelf full of little cakes in pans.

'Give us one,' he begged, 'and then I'll be off.'

'You shall have two,' she said, kneeling down by the oven. 'One for you – mind, it's hot!' He seized it from the cloth and quickly dropped it into his pocket. 'And another, from me,' continued Mary. Taking the second cake, he knelt down and embraced the huddled girl.

'I wants another one,' he whispered.

A quick intelligence swam in her eyes: 'For?'

'Ah, for what's between us, dear Mary.'

The third cake was given him, and they stood up. They moved towards the door. She lifted the latch.

'Good night, my love.' Passively she received his kiss. 'I'll come again to-morrow.'

'No, Frank, don't ever come any more.'

'Aw, I'm coming right enough,' he cried cheerily and confidently as he stepped away.

And I suppose we must conclude that he did.

THE FIELD OF MUSTARD

On a windy afternoon in November they were gathering kindling in the Black Wood, Dinah Lock, Amy Hardwick, and Rose Olliver, three sere disvirgined women from Pollock's Cross. Mrs Lock wore clothes of dull butcher's blue, with a short jacket that affirmed her plumpness, but Rose and Amy had on long grey ulsters. All of them were about forty years old, and the wind and twigs had tousled their gaunt locks, for none had a hat upon her head. They did not go far beyond the margin of the wood, for the forest ahead of them swept high over a hill and was gloomy; behind them the slim trunks of beech, set in a sweet ruin of hoar and scattered leaf, and green briar nimbly fluttering, made a sort of palisade against the light of the open, which was grey, and a wide field of mustard which was yellow. The three women peered up into the trees for dead branches, and when they found any Dinah Lock, the vivacious woman full of shrill laughter, with a bosom as massive as her haunches, would heave up a rope with an iron bolt tied to one end. The bolted end would twine itself around the dead branch, the three women would tug, and after a sharp crack the quarry would fall; as often as not the women would topple over too. By and by they met an old hedger with a round belly belted low, and thin legs tied at each knee, who told them the time by his ancient watch, a stout timepiece which the women sportively admired.

'Come Christmas I'll have me a watch like that!' Mrs Lock called out. The old man looked a little dazed as he fumblingly replaced his chronometer. 'I will,' she continued, 'if the Lord spares me and the pig don't pine.'

'You . . . you don't know what you're talking about,' he said. 'That watch was my uncle's watch.'

'Who was he? I'd like one like it.'

'Was a sergeant-major in the lancers, fought under Sir Garnet Wolseley, and it was given to him.'

'What for?'

The hedger stopped and turned on them, 'Doing of his duty.'

'That all?' cried Dinah Lock. 'Well, I never got no watch for that a-much. Do you know what I see when I went to London? I see'd a watch in a bowl of water, it was glass, and there was a fish swimming round it . . .'

'I don't believe it.'

'There was a fish swimming round it . . .'

'I tell you I don't believe it . . .'

'And the little hand was going on like Clackford Mill. That's the sort of watch I'll have me; none of your Sir Garney Wolsey's!'

'He was a noble Christian man, that was.'

'Ah! I suppose he slept wid Jesus?' yawped Dinah.

'No, he didn't,' the old man disdainfully spluttered. 'He never did. What a God's the matter wid ye?' Dinah cackled with laughter. 'Pah!' he cried, going away, 'great fat thing! Can't tell your guts from your elbows.'

Fifty yards farther on he turned and shouted some obscenity back at them, but they did not heed him; they had begun to make three faggots of the wood they had collected, so he put his fingers to his nose at them and shambled out to the road.

By the time Rose and Dinah were ready, Amy Hardwick, a small slow silent woman, had not finished bundling her faggot together.

'Come on, Amy,' urged Rose.

'Come on,' Dinah said.

'All right, wait a minute,' she replied listlessly.

'O God, that's death!' cried Dinah Lock, and heaving a great faggot to her shoulders she trudged off, followed by Rose with a like burden. Soon they were out of the wood, and crossing a highway they entered a footpath that strayed in a diagonal wriggle to the far corner of the field of mustard. In silence they journeyed until they came to that far corner, where there was a hedged bank. Here they flung their faggots down and sat upon them to wait for Amy Hardwick.

In front of them lay the field they had crossed, a sour scent rising faintly from its yellow blooms that quivered in the wind. Day was dull, the air chill, and the place most solitary. Beyond the field of mustard the eye could see little but forest. There were hills there, a vast curving trunk, but the Black Wood heaved itself effortlessly upon them and lay like a dark pall over the outline of a corpse. Huge and gloomy, the purple woods draped it all completely. A white necklace of a road curved below, where a score of telegraph poles, each crossed with a multitude of white florets, were dwarfed by the hugeness to effigies that resembled hyacinths. Dinah Lock gazed upon this scene whose melancholy, and not its grandeur, had suddenly invaded her; with elbows sunk in her fat thighs, and nursing her cheeks in her hands, she puffed the gloomy air, saying:

'O God, cradle and grave is all there is for we.'

'Where's Amy got to?' asked Rose.

'I could never make a companion of her, you know,' Dinah declared.

'Nor I,' said Rose, 'she's too sour and slow.'

'Her disposition's too serious. Of course, your friends are never what you want them to be, Rose. Sometimes they're better – most often they're worse. But it's such a mercy to have a friend at all; I like you, Rose; I wish you was a man.'

'I might just as well ha' been,' returned the other woman.

'Well, you'd ha' done better; but if you had a tidy little family like me you'd wish you hadn't got 'em.'

'And if you'd never had 'em you'd ha' wished you had.'

'Rose, that's the cussedness of nature, it makes a mock of you. I don't believe it's the Almighty at all, Rose. I'm sure it's the devil, Rose. Dear heart, my corn's a-giving me whatfor; I wonder what that bodes?'

'It's restless weather,' said Rose. She was dark, tall, and not unbeautiful still, though her skin was harsh and her limbs angular. 'Get another month or two over – there's so many of these long dreary hours.'

'Ah, your time's too long, or it's too short, or it's just right but you're too old. Cradle and grave's my portion. Fat old thing he called me!'

Dinah's brown hair was ruffled across her pleasant face and she looked a little forlorn, but corpulence dispossessed her of tragedy. 'I be thin enough a-summertimes, for I lives light and sweats like a bridesmaid, but winters I'm fat as a hog.'

'What all have you to grumble at then?' asked Rose, who had slid to the ground and lay on her stomach staring up at her friend.

'My heart's young, Rose.'

'You've your husband.'

'He's no man at all since he was ill. A long time ill, he was. When he coughed, you know, his insides come up out of him like coffee grouts. Can you ever understand the meaning of that? Coffee! I'm growing old, but my heart's young.'

'So is mine, too: but you got a family, four children grown or growing.' Rose had snapped off a sprig of the mustard flower and was pressing and pulling the bloom in and out of her mouth. 'I've none, and never will have.' Suddenly she sat up, fumbled in her pocket, and produced her purse. She slipped the elastic band from it, and it gaped open. There were a few coins there and a scrap of paper folded. Rose took out the paper and smoothed it open under Dinah's curious gaze. 'I found something lying about at home the other day, and I cut this bit out of it.' In soft tones she began to read:

'The day was void, vapid; time itself seemed empty. Come evening it rained softly. I sat by my fire turning over the leaves of a book, and I was dejected, until I came upon a little old-fashioned engraving at the bottom of a page. It imaged a procession of some angelic children in a garden, little placidly-naked substantial babes, with tiny bird-wings. One carried a bow, others a horn of plenty, or a hamper of fruit, or a set of reedpipes. They were garlanded and full of grave joys. And at the sight of them a strange bliss flowed into me such as I had never known, and I thought this world was all a garden, though its light was hidden and its children not yet born.'

Rose did not fold the paper up; she crushed it in her hand and lay down again without a word.

'Huh, I tell you, Rose, a family's a torment. I never wanted
mine. God love, Rose, I'd lay down my life for 'em; I'd cut myself
into fourpenny pieces so they shouldn't come to harm; if one of
'em was to die I'd sorrow to my grave. But I know, I know, I
know I never wanted 'em, they were not for me, I was just an
excuse for their blundering into the world. Somehow I've been
duped, and every woman born is duped so, one ways or another
in the end. I had my sport with my man, but I ought never to
have married. Now I'd love to begin all over again, and as God's
my maker, if it weren't for those children, I'd be gone off out
into the world again tomorrow, Rose. But I dunno what 'ud
become o' me.'

The wind blew strongly athwart the yellow field, and the
odour of mustard rushed upon the brooding women. Protestingly
the breeze flung itself upon the forest; there was a gliding cry
among the rocking pinions as of some lost wave seeking a
forgotten shore. The angular faggot under Dinah Lock had
begun to vex her; she too sunk to the ground and lay beside Rose
Olliver, who asked:

'And what 'ud become of your old man?'

For a few moments Dinah Lock paused. She too took a sprig
of the mustard and fondled it with her lips. 'He's no man now,
the illness feebled him, and the virtue's gone; no man at all since
two years, and bald as a piece of cheese – I like a hairy man, like
. . . do you remember Rufus Blackthorn, used to be gamekeeper
here?'

Rose stopped playing with her flower. 'Yes, I knew Rufus
Blackthorn.'

'A fine bold man that was! Never another like him herea-
bouts, not in England neither; not in the whole world – though
I've heard some queer talk of those foreigners, Australians,
Chinymen. Well!'

'Well?' said Rose.

'He was a devil.' Dinah Lock began to whisper. 'A perfect devil; I can't say no fairer than that. I wish I could, but I can't.'

'O come,' protested Rose, 'he was a kind man. He'd never see anybody want for a thing.'

'No,' there was playful scorn in Dinah's voice; 'he'd shut his eyes first!'

'Not to a woman he wouldn't, Dinah.'

'Ah! Well – perhaps – he was good to women.'

'I can tell you things as would surprise you,' murmured Rose.

'You! But – well no, no. I could tell *you* things as you wouldn't believe. Me and Rufus! We was – O my – yes!'

'He *was* handsome.'

'O, a pretty man!' Dinah acceded warmly. 'Black as coal and bold as a fox. I'd been married nigh on ten years when he first set foot in these parts. I'd got three children then. He used to give me a saucy word whenever he saw me, for I liked him and he knew it. One Whitsun Monday I was home all alone, the children were gone somewheres, and Tom was away boozing. I was putting some plants in our garden – I loved a good flower in those days – I wish the world was all a garden, but now my Tom he digs 'em up, digs everything up proper and never puts 'em back. Why, we had a crocus, once! And as I was doing that planting someone walked by the garden in such a hurry. I looked up and there was Rufus, all dressed up to the nines, and something made me call out to him. "Where be you off to in that flaming hurry," I says. "Going to a wedding," says he. "Shall I come with 'ee?" I says. "Ah yes," he says, very glad; "but hurry up, for I be sharp set and all." So I run in-a-doors and popped on my things and off we went to Jim Pickering's wedding over at Clackford Mill. When Jim brought the bride home from church that Rufus got hold of a gun and fired it off up chimney, and

down come soot, the bushels of it! All over the room, and a
chimney-pot burst and rattled down the tiles into a p'rambulator.
What a rumbullion that was! But no one got angry – there was
plenty of drink and we danced all the afternoon. Then we come
home together again through the woods. O lord – I said to myself
– I shan't come out with you ever again, and that's what I said to
Rufus Blackthorn. But I did, you know! I woke up in bed that
night, and the moon shone on me dreadful – I thought the place
was afire. But there was Tom snoring, and I lay and thought of
me and Rufus in the wood, till I could have jumped out into the
moonlight, stark, and flown over the chimney. I didn't sleep any
more. And I saw Rufus the next night, and the night after that,
often, often. Whenever I went out I left Tom the cupboardful –
that's all he troubled about. I was mad after Rufus, and while
that caper was on I couldn't love my husband. No.'

'No?' queried Rose.

'Well, I pretended I was ill, and I took my young Katey to
sleep with me, and give Tom her bed. He didn't seem to mind,
but after a while I found he was gallivanting after other women.
Course, I soon put a stopper on that. And then – what do you
think? Bless me if Rufus weren't up to the same tricks? Deep as
the sea, that man. Faithless, you know, but such a bold one.'

Rose lay silent, plucking wisps of grass; there was a wry smile
on her face.

'Did ever he tell you the story of the man who was drowned?'
she asked at length. Dinah shook her head. Rose continued.
'Before he came here he was keeper over in that Oxfordshire,
where the river goes right through the woods, and he slept in a
boathouse moored to the bank. Some gentleman was drowned
near there, an accident it was, but they couldn't find the body.
So they offered a reward of ten pound for it to be found . . .'

'Ten, ten pounds!'

'Yes. Well, all the watermen said the body wouldn't come up for ten days . . .'

'No more they do.'

'It didn't. And so late one night – it was moonlight – some men in a boat kept on hauling and poking round the house where Rufus was, and he heard 'em say 'It must be here, it must be here,' and Rufus shouts out to them, 'Course he's here! I got him in bed with me!''

'Aw!' chuckled Dinah.

'Yes, and next day he got the ten pounds, because he *had* found the body and hidden it away.'

'Feared nothing,' said Dinah, 'nothing at all; he'd have been rude to Satan. But he was very delicate with his hands, sewing and things like that. I used to say to him, "Come, let me mend your coat," or whatever it was, but he never would, always did such things of himself. "I don't allow no female to patch my clothes," he'd say, " 'cos they works with a red-hot needle and a burning thread." And he used to make fine little slippers out of reeds.'

'Yes,' Rose concurred, 'he made me a pair.'

'You!' Dinah cried. 'What – were you . . .?'

Rose turned her head away. 'We was all cheap to him,' she said softly, 'cheap as old rags; we was like chaff before him.'

Dinah Lock lay still, very still, ruminating; but whether in old grief or new rancour Rose was not aware, and she probed no further. Both were quiet, voiceless, recalling the past delirium. They shivered, but did not rise. The wind increased in the forest, its hoarse breath sorrowed in the yellow field, and swift masses of cloud flowed and twirled in a sky without end and full of gloom.

'Hallo!' cried a voice, and there was Amy beside them, with a faggot almost overwhelming her. 'Shan't stop now,' she said, 'for

I've got this faggot perched just right, and I shouldn't ever get it up again. I found a shilling in the 'ood, you,' she continued shrilly and gleefully. 'Come along to my house after tea, and we'll have a quart of stout.'

'A shilling, Amy!' cried Rose.

'Yes,' called Mrs Hardwick, trudging steadily on. 'I tried to find the fellow to it, but no more luck. Come and wet it after tea!'

'Rose,' said Dinah, 'come on.' She and Rose with much circumstance heaved up their faggots and tottered after, but by then Amy was turned out of sight down the little lane to Pollock's Cross.

'Your children will be home,' said Rose as they went along, 'they'll be looking out for you.'

'Ah, they'll want their bellies filling!'

'It must be lovely a-winter's nights, you setting round your fire with 'em, telling tales, and brushing their hair.'

'Ain't you got a fire of your own indoors,' grumbled Dinah.

'Yes.'

'Well, why don't you set by it then!' Dinah's faggot caught the briars of a hedge that overhung, and she tilted round with a mild oath. A covey of partridges feeding beyond scurried away with ruckling cries. One foolish bird dashed into the telegraph wires and dropped dead.

'They're good children, Dinah, yours are. And they make you a valentine, and give you a ribbon on your birthday, I expect?'

'They're naught but a racket from cockcrow till the old man snores – and then it's worse!'

'Oh, but the creatures, Dinah!'

'You . . . you got your quiet trim house, and only your man to look after, a kind man, and you'll set with him in the evenings and play your dominoes or your draughts, and he'll look at you – the nice man – over the board and stroke your hand now and again.'

The wind hustled the two women closer together, and as they stumbled under their burdens Dinah Lock stretched out a hand and touched the other woman's arm. 'I like you, Rose, I wish you was a man.'

Rose did not reply. Again they were quiet, voiceless, and thus in fading light they came to their homes. But how windy, dispossessed and ravaged, roved the darkening world! Clouds were borne frantically across the heavens, as if in a rout of battle, and the lovely earth seemed to sigh in grief at some calamity all unknown to men.